Lady Fortescue Steps Out

Being the first volume of The Poor Relation

M.C. Beaton

Canvas

Constable & Robinson Ltd.
55–56 Russell Square
London WC1B 4HP
www.constablerobinson.com

First published in the US by St Martin's Press, 1992

First published in the UK by Canvas,
an imprint of Constable & Robinson Ltd., 2013

A copy of the British Library Cataloguing in
Publication Data is available from the British Library

ISBN: 978-1-78033-317-5 (paperback)
IBN: 978-1-47210-486-1 (ebook)

Typeset by TW Typesetting, Plymouth, Devon

Printed and bound by CPI Group (UK) Ltd, Croydon, CR0 4YY

1 3 5 7 9 10 8 6 4 2

M. C. Beaton is the author of the hugely successful Agatha Raisin and Hamish Macbeth series, as well as a quartet of Edwardian murder mysteries featuring heroine Lady Rose Summer, several Regency romance series and a stand-alone murder mystery, *The Skeleton in the Closet* – all published by Constable & Robinson. She left a full-time career in journalism to turn to writing, and now divides her time between the Cotswolds and Paris. Visit www.mcbeatonbooks.co.uk for more, or follow M. C. Beaton on Twitter: @mc_beaton.

*For Ann Robinson and her daughter,
Emma Wilson, with love.*

ONE

It is a melancholy truth that even great men have their poor relations.

CHARLES DICKENS

In the Regency, in an age when gambling had reached ridiculous heights and the aristocracy spent and wasted money as never before, there were many poor in London, miserable, half-starved, ragged creatures.

But there were also the members of the invisible poor, the victims of genteel poverty who, with many subterfuges and stratagems, hid their condition from the eyes of polite society.

The poor relations of aristocrats who lived in London led a lonely and dreary existence, living on the charity of their noble relatives; or on some meagre allowance from a family trust. Once a year, they were taken out and dusted down and conveyed to some stately home where they made themselves as inconspicuous as possible, hoping to be ignored, hoping that regular meals and fires would last as long as possible. But the day would always come when they were packed up and delivered back to London and a life of genteel cold and hunger. What kept them from helping each other, what kept them apart, was pride.

A small section of this miserable horde would have joined its fellows in dying, lonely and forgotten, had it not been for one momentous May day in Hyde Park when old Lady Fortescue met Colonel Sandhurst.

Lady Fortescue lived in a tall house in Bond Street. The house was nearly all she had left and she stubbornly held onto it. She had just reached her seventieth year, a great age in the days of the Regency, when very few managed to achieve the biblical figure of three score years and ten.

She had just returned from a humiliating visit to her nephew, the Duke of Rowcester. Two heavy silver candlesticks belonging to the duke had been found in her trunk. In vain had she pleaded her innocence, in vain had she protested loudly and with many oaths that she did not know how they had come to be among her effects – she was asked to leave.

The fact that she had actually stolen them did not ease her pain. It was the first time she had stooped to crime. The candlesticks had been standing on a table in a little-used side room. She had been so sure that nobody would miss them. And so she had taken them, thinking gleefully of all the meals the silver sticks would bring her when she returned to London and sold them. But their disappearance had been noticed immediately. While everyone was accusing everyone else, for the great mansion was full of guests, the duke had quietly dispatched a posse of servants to search the rooms. He had not made her humiliation public. He had simply taken her aside and told her the candlesticks had been found and that his carriage would be ready to convey her back to London in two hours' time. He had listened to her protestations of innocence for a time and then had cut them short by saying wearily, 'Theft is a bad enough crime. Do not make it worse by lying.' And that was that.

Lady Fortescue was a tall woman with white hair and snapping black eyes. Her skin was dead white and her mouth thin and always rouged a bright scarlet. Although her husband had been dead for twenty years, she had never put off her mourning weeds. She had two servants – Betty, who was fifty-nine, and John, who was sixty. She could not remember when she had last been able to pay them a wage. But they stayed with her, for there was nowhere else for them to go.

Her humiliation had taken place in February and since then she had hidden in her house, too ashamed to go out, frightened that the criminal she had become would be evident for all to see. But one beautiful May day, she became weary of the dark house and of herself and her shame and decided to go and take the air in Hyde Park. When she got there, she sat down on a bench in the sun, a grim black figure, back ramrod-straight, one hand leaning on the ivory handle of her parasol.

3

She looked thoughtfully at that parasol. The ivory handle was mounted in silver. As she looked at it, it became transformed in her mind's eye into a pile of savoury meat pies. How odd, she thought, giving herself a mental shake, that all the little knick-knacks of a lady's wardrobe, once taken for granted, should now be considered as so many pawnable items to get money for food and coals. Unlike most elderly people, she craved food rather than warmth, for she had always enjoyed a hearty appetite.

The sunlight seemed to intensify her loneliness. She sat there for a long time. The fashionable hour came and went, with its glitter and carriages and horses. Still she sat as the Park became silent again and long shadows from the trees crept over the grass like so many dark fingers of doom pointing the way to the grave.

An elderly man was approaching the bench on which she was seated, striding out down the walk. She had seen him before. Like herself, he was tall and white-haired. His clothes were worn and his boots were in need of repair and he was surely as old as she, but he carried himself with an air, an old-fashioned hat called a wideawake tilted rakishly to one side on top of his carefully curled and pomaded hair.

He was almost abreast of her when he suddenly put his hand to his brow and then collapsed at her feet in a dead faint.

Lady Fortescue looked around for help but there was no one to be seen. She knelt down beside the

4

fallen gentleman and, taking her smelling-salts out of her reticule, held them under his nose. His eyes fluttered open. They were very blue, childlike eyes to be set in such an old face.

'My apologies, ma'am,' he said faintly. 'Must be on m'way to my club.'

Lady Fortescue's sharp eyes took in the details of genteel poverty, from well-pressed but worn clothes and split gloves to cracked boots, and said, to her own surprise, 'Sit down with me for a little, sir.'

She helped him to the bench. He again apologized, saying lightly that illness was one of the problems of old age.

Lady Fortescue would, before her disastrous visit to her nephew, have accepted this polite fiction and the gentleman would have got to his feet and gone on his way, and that would have been that.

But her own humiliation was still fresh in her mind and suddenly she found herself rebelling against all the shifts and scrapes to maintain appearances and said bluntly, 'You need food.'

He looked at her, appalled at the enormity of what she had said. 'My dear lady,' he remarked, his voice still light and pleasant, 'I am amazed at you. How can you say such a thing? But let me present myself. I am Colonel Sandhurst, late of the 147th.'

She bent her head, a stately acknowledgement of the introduction, and said with an edge in her voice, 'Oh, go on your way, then, sirrah. But have you ever thought that here we sit, both of us genteelly poor and wasting a lot of time trying to hide the fact? And

5

there are others like us who come here, for the recognizable and unfashionable poor are not allowed in Hyde Park, and because no one is going to charge us for breathing the air or looking at the trees. No, stay a moment!' For he had started to rise. 'I am Lady Fortescue. I have decided to tell you what happened to me recently and then, if you like, you can walk away.'

The colonel listened gravely, and as she told him of the theft of the candlesticks a thin mist began to veil the trees and a curious squirrel stopped at their feet to stare up at them with bright, inquisitive eyes.

After she had finished, he sat in silence for a long time, and then he slowly removed his hat and held it to his breast as if about to mourn the passing of genteel pretensions.

'Lady Fortescue,' he said, 'I am *very* hungry.'

'Yes, I thought you might be,' she said brusquely. 'Come home with me. My Betty has a mutton pie and some broth.'

When Lady Fortescue eventually stopped outside her home in Bond Street, the colonel looked up at the tall building curiously, imagining she rented one of the rooms. She led the way into a fine hallway, although it was devoid of furniture, and said, 'Leave your hat on the knob on the banisters. I hope you do not mind. We will eat in the kitchen with my servants. The few coals I am able to afford are for the kitchen fire and it is silly to sit in the cold of the dining room. Although the weather has turned warm, it has not yet permeated into the house.'

Surprised that she obviously owned the whole house, the colonel followed her down a narrow flight of stairs to the kitchen. The servant, Betty, was a thin, bent, swarthy woman, like a gypsy. She dropped a curtsy and concealed her obvious surprise when her mistress announced, 'We have a guest for dinner.'

'I'll just lay two places in the dining room, my lady,' said Betty.

'No need for that. The kitchen is warm. We will eat here. Set two places at this end of the table and you and John may eat at the other. Where is John?'

'He went out to look for some firewood, my lady. A building fell down in Holborn, so he heard, and he went off to see if he could take some of the house timber.'

'I hope he is not caught,' said Lady Fortescue equably. 'Pray be seated, Colonel. I am afraid we can only offer you beer – wine, tea and coffee being much too expensive.'

The kitchen door opened and a thickset man came in with a sack on his back. 'Got some wood, my lady,' he said gruffly, 'and would have got more had the watch not come along.' Then he saw the colonel and looked startled.

'You need not stand on ceremony with Colonel Sandhurst, John,' said Lady Fortescue. 'But as we have an unaccustomed guest, I suggest you build up the kitchen fire for this night.'

Soon the colonel was drinking a bowl of broth while a bright fire crackled up the kitchen chimney. Betty and John, as instructed, sat at the far end of the table and talked in low voices to each other, and so, emboldened by hot broth and strong beer, the colonel began to tell his story. All he had was his army pension. His next payment was not due for another month. But he had been so sure that his rich cousin John would invite him on a visit that he had spent what he had left. The invitation had not come as it had always done in the past, and so he had no money left to buy anything.

Betty rose and took away his empty bowl and then produced a steaming mutton pie from the oven. The colonel thought almost tearfully that nothing in his life ever before had tasted so marvellous as that pie, with floury potatoes and a generous helping of pease-pudding.

'Eat slowly, now,' cautioned Lady Fortescue. She was beginning to enjoy herself. She had been so very lonely. Such a long time ago, when she had been able to keep a full staff of servants, Betty had been a housemaid and John a footman. When she had fallen on hard times, they said they would stay on provided she gave them permission to marry. That permission seemed to bind them to her in loyalty. But they were devoted to each other and often made Lady Fortescue feel like an intruder in her own house.

'Forgive me for saying so, Lady Fortescue,' ventured the colonel, 'but would not your circumstances be easier if you sold this place?'

'It is all I have to remind me of my late husband,' said Lady Fortescue. 'I shall leave in my coffin.'

The evening wore on. The colonel seemed rejuvenated by warmth and company. He talked of books he had read and plays he had seen; he laughed over all the pathetic shifts he had made to keep up appearances, and while he talked, Lady Fortescue began to get the glimmerings of a great idea.

When he at last fell silent, she said slowly, 'You have a small allowance from the army and I have a small allowance from a family trust. There is a great deal of space in this house and you have said that at present you are paying for your lodgings. Why not move in here with me?'

'My dear lady!'

'Why not?' demanded Lady Fortescue. 'We could pool our resources. We are too old for such an arrangement to cause either scandal or comment.'

The colonel looked around slowly at the cheerful kitchen. 'It is certainly an idea. Yes, by George! We could play cards of an evening. And talk.' He threw his arms wide and laughed. 'I have not talked so long in this age.'

The great idea burst full in all its glory in Lady Fortescue's head.

'And,' she said calmly, 'when we are settled together, we shall go out into London Town and find others like ourselves.'

'But that is ridiculous,' he expostulated.

'If it is not ridiculous in your case, sir, why should it be ridiculous in the case of anyone else? Think on it. An army of poor relations!'

'You are an amazing woman,' he cried. He shook his head and then suddenly capitulated. 'What has either of us got to lose?'

Lady Fortescue took him on a tour of the house. It was, he reflected, much larger than he would have guessed from the outside. There were a multitude of rooms, with light patches on the damp-stained wallpaper showing where pictures and mirrors had once hung.

'There is very little furniture,' said Lady Fortescue. 'I sold it off, bit by bit, over the years, then the paintings went, then the ornaments.' She sighed as she opened another door. 'But here is my husband's bedroom. I had not the heart to sell off anything here, so you may consider it as your own.' While the colonel admired the handsome four-poster bed and tall wardrobe, she went to the window and threw open the shutters. 'The night is mild,' she said. 'Not like winter. You have no need of coals at present. There is no need for delay. You may move in this night. Do you have a great deal of stuff to bring?'

'No, Lady Fortescue. Like you, I have been selling off everything bit by bit. What I have can be brought round on a handcart.'

'Then I will send John with you. He can borrow the cart from the tavern next door. Then rest, and we will start within the next few days on our search.'

He raised her hand to his lips and said, 'You are an angel. Forget about that wretched nephew of yours.'

'Why not?' laughed Lady Fortescue. 'I am sure he has forgotten my very existence!'

But the Duke of Rowcester had not. In fact, he was thinking of his aunt at that very moment. The whole affair of the candlesticks had puzzled him. But he had decided at last that, like some elderly people, Lady Fortescue had begun to lose her wits. She probably had taken the candlesticks in a fit of mental aberration and then forgotten about them. He should not have sent her packing in that way. Perhaps, were he married, a wife would have handled the business with more tact.

He was thirty-three and had never married. He had inherited the dukedom at an early age and the responsibility had left him with little time to enjoy himself, as his father, the late duke, had let everything on his vast estates go to rack and ruin. Now that all was running well – in fact, had been for some years now – the duke was still reluctant to go to that famous marriage market, the London Season, to look for a bride. Because he was a duke and accounted handsome, he knew he could get any woman he wanted, and so, when any pretty young miss smiled on him, he cynically assumed she was smiling on his title and fortune.

There had been only one, some time ago, at a ball in Grosvenor Square, a beauty with green eyes like emeralds and midnight-black hair. He remembered her gaiety and wit. But after the ball she seemed to have dropped out of the bottom of the world. Her name had been Harriet James, he remembered that well. But she and her family had simply disappeared from the social scene and no one seemed to know what had happened to them.

He thought again of Lady Fortescue and shifted uncomfortably. Perhaps on his next visit to town he would call on her to see how she went on.

Mrs Budley, one very sad widow, was sitting in Hyde Park, crying into a wisp of lace handkerchief as Lady Fortescue passed on the arm of Colonel Sandhurst. 'Do you think . . . ?' began the colonel.

'No, I do not think,' said Lady Fortescue. 'Too young by half.'

Mrs Budley cried on. She did not know what to do. Her servants had all walked out on her that morning and the reason she had fled to Hyde Park, leaving her house by the back entrance, was because of the duns at the front. Her carefree husband, Jack, had gambled and drunk himself into an early grave two years before. She was amazingly pretty, and fashionably dressed, with a trim figure and neat ankles, she looked much younger than the thirty years old that she actually was. She had a sweet face and pansy-brown eyes and fluffy brown hair and a fluffy mind to go with it, and she did not know which way to turn. She had written to her own relations and to Jack's for aid, but only one had offered to help, and that help took the form of an invitation to stay at Christmas, and Christmas seemed a lifetime away.

Her parents had died shortly after her marriage and she had neither brothers nor sisters. She felt like a lost child. Only the day before, a certain Sir Giles Marrin had suggested to her a way of meeting her debts, but the way suggested was for her to become his mistress and she had recoiled in horror from his bloated face and clutching hands.

She cried harder at the thought of Sir Giles.

'My dear lady, I cannot bear it,' came a masculine voice from somewhere above her head and a woman's voice answered, 'I tell you, she's too young. Probably lost her pet poodle. Come away.'

Mrs Eliza Budley looked up through a mist of tears and saw a blurred picture of two tall, elderly people staring down at her.

The gentleman raised his hat and said gently, 'Colonel Sandhurst at your service, ma'am. You are in sore distress.'

'No one can help me,' said Mrs Budley wildly. 'No one. I am ruined.'

Some sort of silent agreement passed between the elderly pair and they sat down on either side of her. 'Why don't you tell us about it,' said Colonel Sandhurst. 'This is Lady Fortescue, a highly intelligent and reliable prop.'

Lady Fortescue suppressed a snort of laughter at being called a reliable prop, and then it dawned on her with surprise that in the few days she had known the colonel, she always seemed to be laughing at something. This made her more charitable towards the pretty little thing next to her, and so she pressed Mrs Budley's mittened hand and begged her to unburden herself.

And so, between sobs, Mrs Budley did, ending up with the tale of Sir Giles.

'You are not quite what we were looking for,' said

Lady Fortescue. 'You are fashionably gowned and well fed.' She explained how she and Colonel Sandhurst had joined forces. 'You see,' she explained, 'I live in a large gloomy house and we share our food with my servants. A young lady as pretty as yourself will soon marry again . . .'

'I am thirty,' said Mrs Budley, 'and have no dowry.'

Lady Fortescue looked down at her curiously. 'Do you think you would like to live with an old pair such as myself and Colonel Sandhurst? No balls or parties or theatres. Just cards of an evening. We live simply and share everything, but we owe nothing.'

'I would love that,' said Mrs Budley. 'But how can I get away from the duns?'

'Do you own your house?' asked the colonel.

'Yes, but it is mortgaged to the hilt!'

'Do you own the furniture?'

'Yes, although I have sold all my jewellery.'

'Then it is quite simple,' said the colonel. 'Lady Fortescue's servant will hire a cart. You will need to sell a piece of furniture or some gowns or something to pay for the hire, Mrs Budley. Then at nightfall, Lady Fortescue's servant will take the cart to your house, where we will load it with the furniture and your belongings. The duns can fight over the ownership of the house in the morning.'

Mrs Budley's tears dried as if by magic. 'Do you mean I will be *safe* from them?'

'Oh, yes. But as you have no servants, and Lady Fortescue's John is quite old, I am afraid you must

14

demean yourself to help carry some of the lighter items. In fact, you must return and try to find something to sell so that, along with the cart, we can hire two strong men.'

Mrs Budley's face fell ludicrously. 'Apart from furniture, I do not know if I have anything left to sell. And it will be very hard for me to carry anything out with the duns on the doorstep.'

'We will come with you,' said Lady Fortescue firmly. 'I have been a long time poor, and it will amaze you what can be sold.'

Mrs Budley's house was in Clarence Square. She led the way in through the back garden and opened the kitchen door.

Lady Fortescue went from cellar to attic, feeling stronger and more cheerful than she had done in ages. The house was fully furnished. It would take several cartloads. The kitchen was full of pots and crockery and the larder full of stores. What a haul! And she had thought the colonel an old fool when he had first suggested approaching Mrs Budley.

But the thing to do was to find something easily portable to sell to pay for the removal.

It was the colonel who found a silver snuff-box at the back of a drawer in the late Mr Budley's bedroom.

By dawn the next day, Mrs Budley's furniture was spread throughout the rooms of the house in Bond Street and the contents of her kitchen were delighting Betty and John. The colonel and Lady Fortescue were exhausted but triumphant when they finally crawled off to bed.

Mrs Budley went to her own bed, which had been brought on the cart along with all the other furniture, put her hand under her cheek, and fell into a dreamless sleep, her last waking thought that it was wonderful to be taken care of.

Although Lady Fortescue pointed out that they could live on the little widow's possessions for some time, she said that her conscience would not allow her to take advantage of such a feckless little creature who was far too trusting and simple for her own good. The colonel agreed. So after several pleasant days of dinners served once more in a dining room which had possessed only one long table and two chairs and now was augmented by Mrs Budley's dining chairs, and after several nights of quiet sleep, Lady Fortescue and Colonel Sandhurst set out once more to Hyde Park.

The weather was still fine and the colonel walked with a spring in his step. The money he had got from the sale of the snuff-box had not only paid for the furniture removal but had left him with quite a comfortable little sum of money. He longed for a new pair of boots but instead he duly entered the money in a new accounts book supplied by Lady Fortescue. Every penny must be divided up, but not until they felt more secure.

They started hopefully enough, but by the end of the afternoon were beginning to feel dejected and weary. They had approached various people who were obviously in a state of genteel poverty and had been rebuffed haughtily by them all.

'Let 'em rot,' said Lady Fortescue with sudden venom. 'There's roast beef for dinner tonight and a bottle of damn good claret from Mrs Budley's cellar.'

'Look over there!' said the colonel. 'That female by the water. Looks as if she might jump in.'

'Probably some madwoman,' said Lady Fortescue. 'Very well. We'll try her, but no more this day!'

Miss Tonks walked along by the waters of the Serpentine and wondered if she could find the courage to throw herself in. A dead dog surfaced and floated past pathetically, its feet in the air, and she recoiled with a little cry.

She was so very hungry, and yet the pains inside her were caused by grief. She was a vague, indeterminate woman of forty who had been dealt the first severe blow of her life five years ago, when her beloved parents had died and left everything to her elder sister. Crushed, hardly able to believe that her parents had not left her anything, Miss Tonks was forced to live in a small room and live on a pittance, supplied to her quarterly by her sister. Her sister often invited Miss Tonks to stay and Miss Tonks went, for it meant food and warmth and elegance, although her sister, Honoria, always seemed to find humiliating little tasks for her to do, like mending stockings. And when guests were invited for dinner, Miss Tonks was expected to eat her meals on a tray in her room.

Then, only a short time ago, her bleak existence had been lit up by pure romance. A handsome young man of twenty-five began to court her. She was dazzled, she was charmed, she spent what she had of her allowance on buying him trinkets. The romance flared across the dreary skies of her life like a comet. And then he had told her he had a gambling debt he could not meet and asked her for five hundred pounds. Amazed that he had not guessed her circumstances, she told him how little she had and after that, she had never seen him again.

Now she was broken-hearted and hungry.

She threw her arms up to the sky in a tragicomic gesture of despair and cried aloud, 'I am one of life's worms.'

'And why do you say that?' asked a calm voice behind her.

Miss Tonks swung round, blushing. An elderly couple were standing, watching her steadily.

'I w-was rehearsing for . . . for amateur dramatics,' she stammered.

The lady looked at her coldly. The gentleman bowed. The lady said, 'I am sorry. We are only interested in people in trouble.'

Miss Tonks would have remained silent had not the colonel removed his hat and said gently, 'We know what it is to be poor. We were wondering if we could be of help to you.'

Convention warred with a desire for help in Miss Tonks's flat bosom. One did not speak of money, one kept up appearances; a lady never, on any occasion . . .

'Oh, help me,' she said, 'I don't know what to do.'

'Come and sit down with us on that bench over

there,' said Lady Fortescue. 'I am Lady Fortescue and this is Colonel Sandhurst, and you are . . . ?'

'Miss Letitia Tonks, my lady.'

Again the conventions nearly sealed Miss Tonks's thin lips for good, but the Park appeared deserted and there was only this odd couple. She began to speak, slowly at first, and then the words came tumbling out.

'Dear me,' said Lady Fortescue when she had finished, 'men were deceivers ever . . . apart from Colonel Sandhurst, that is. I will explain why we are here.' She told the amazed Miss Tonks of how they had planned to find other 'poor relations' so that they might all band together and share their resources.

'But I have nothing to offer,' wailed Miss Tonks. 'I have already spent my allowance.'

'But you will have it soon again,' pointed out Lady Fortescue. 'I suggest you repair to my home in Bond Street with us and partake of a dish of roast beef.'

Harriet James watched them go. She herself had seen that odd woman pacing up and down by the water, and had wondered whether to approach her or not. Then that elderly couple had gone up to her. As they had passed her, the gentleman had said gently, 'A good slice of roast beef is the best medicine I know,' and the tall elderly lady had laughed, a clear, bell-like sound.

Roast beef, thought Harriet wistfully, as her stomach gave an unmaidenly rumble. Then she went home to a supper of bread and cheese.

19

TWO

O world! how apt the poor are to be proud.
WILLIAM SHAKESPEARE

The following day, Harriet James decided to call on her friend, Mrs Budley. She had met Mrs Budley by chance a month ago while walking in the Park. They had talked of this and that and Mrs Budley had invited Harriet back to her home for tea. They were unable to go in by the front door because of the duns. Mrs Budley had been blushing and embarrassed as she had led Harriet round the back. But she did not refer to the duns hammering at the door, nor to the surliness of her servants. Harriet saw nothing wrong in this. Ladies always kept up appearances and did not talk of money or the lack of it.

She had called a couple of times after that only to be told that Mrs Budley was 'not at home'. This could well be interpreted as 'Mrs Budley does not want to see you', but after calm reflection, Harriet decided that Mrs Budley, under pressure from the duns, had simply told her servants to tell all that she was 'not at home'.

To her dismay, the house had the shutters up. She

inquired at the neighbouring house and was told by the butler that Mrs Budley had run away from her debts, taking all her belongings during the night and leaving the house to the duns.

Depressed, Harriet turned her steps towards the Park. Oh, Hyde Park! Glittering show-place for the carriage classes and refuge for the genteel poor!

Life had once been infinitely better for Harriet. Her parents had rented a town house with a view to launching Harriet on the London Season. Although they were neither fashionable nor rich, they were sure that Harriet's startling beauty would soon secure a wealthy husband.

Her very first ball was an amazing success. Had not London's most sought-after bachelor, the Duke of Rowcester, asked her for two whole dances? They had danced a waltz. Somehow, on balmy days like this, Harriet could still hear the lilting music in her head and see his handsome, hard profile and the caressing warmth in his grey eyes as he had looked down at her.

But in the early hours of the following morning, her father had suffered an apoplexy. Her mother had decided the only thing to do was to remove him back to the pure air of the country and his own doctor. And so they had left. Mr James had only lived another month and his grieving widow followed him to the grave a year later.

It was then that Harriet found out the extent of their debts. With the help of the family lawyer, she had sold the house and estate and paid everyone off. There was very little left.

She returned to London and found rented accommodation in Bayswater. Occasionally she wrote to one of her relatives and often secured an invitation to stay, but such visits were humiliating. She was neither fish nor fowl, neither guest nor servant. In despair, she tried to find a post as a governess, but her beauty apparently made her unemployable. Hyde Park became a sort of second home. She knew all the regulars by sight – that is, the people on foot like herself.

She entered by the lodge and set out over the grass, wearing a serviceable black gown and hat. Most of her frivolous ballgowns and fashionable dresses had been sold, leaving her with only a basic wardrobe.

And then she saw, walking sedately along one of the walks, like a family party, the tall, white-haired military-looking man, the severe elderly lady on his arm. Behind them walked Mrs Budley, and with her was that odd spinster creature who had so recently looked as if she were about to plunge into the waters of the Serpentine.

Harriet hailed Mrs Budley and curtsied to the party. 'I called at your address,' said Harriet to Mrs Budley, 'but you had left.'

'I am now residing in Bond Street,' said Mrs Budley. 'Lady Fortescue, may I present Miss James. Miss James, Lady Fortescue, Miss Tonks and Colonel Sandhurst.'

Harriet curtsied again and looked at them curiously.

Then Harriet noticed the colonel nudge Lady

Fortescue, and Lady Fortescue give a little shake of her head.

'We must be on our way, Miss James,' said Lady Fortescue.

Harriet looked at Mrs Budley. 'May I call on you?'

Lady Fortescue frowned and Mrs Budley said with a little gasp, 'It is not very convenient at the moment, Miss James.'

Feeling depressed, Harriet made to move on past them. A shaft of sunlight struck through the trees and highlighted a neat darn on Harriet's gown. 'And no maid either,' said Lady Fortescue. 'Stay a moment, Miss James. Your beauty blinded me to the condition of your clothes.'

'I beg your pardon!' exclaimed Harriet.

'Oh, do listen,' said Mrs Budley, clapping her hands. 'The veriest thing! They are going to ask you too.'

In the clear autocratic tones of the old aristocracy, Lady Fortescue outlined the workings of what she bluntly called the Poor Relations Club.

Harriet listened intently. Here were her own kind. What a simply wonderful idea! What was it that made the life of the genteel poor so miserable? Why, false pride.

'Do let me come with you,' Harriet found herself begging. 'I do not have much to offer, but I could keep the accounts for you. I am clever with figures.'

'Very well,' said Lady Fortescue. 'Do you have a house to sell?'

'No, my lady. I rent a room and the furniture is also rented. What I have can be carried.'

'We will repair to Bond Street and you may give my John your address and then go with him. We also must sit down and discuss the matter of my servants.' Her hand went to her bosom to look at her fob-watch, and then as usual she remembered she had pawned it. 'I feel it must be about time for tea. We have tea, Miss James, thanks to Mrs Budley's kitchen supplies. My Betty was not trained as a cook, but she does good plain meals and has promised scones, and we even have butter. Dear me, I have not tasted fresh butter this age.'

She and the colonel moved forward, and with an odd feeling of being back at school, Harriet fell into line behind them with Mrs Budley and Miss Tonks. 'It is all very odd,' she whispered. 'Is it comfortable? Does it work?'

'We are like a family,' said Mrs Budley. 'And so safe! My servants walked out on me, Miss James, and you know how awful it is to walk out in public unescorted. The gentlemen do plague one so.'

Miss Tonks looked wistful. That was one of the few indignities she had not had to suffer.

As they approached Bond Street, Harriet reflected that it was a street she would never have walked down on her own. The gentlemen regarded it as their own preserve, rather like St James's Street.

The hall when they entered was now furnished with a handsome side-table, courtesy of Mrs Budley. 'I shall tell Betty to bring the tea to the dining room, for we must have a discussion,' said Lady Fortescue.

Soon they were all in the dining room, drinking

tea and eating hot buttered scones, Harriet trying very hard not to gulp hers down.

'Now,' said Lady Fortescue, adjusting a frivolous lace cap on her snowy hair, 'Betty and John, take seats at the end of the table. This concerns you.' She looked around at the others. 'Betty and John here have served me well, and still do. They are old, although John is still very strong,' she went on in that way the aristocracy had of discussing servants as if they were blind and deaf. 'The fact is that this is a large house and there are now five of us. It is as well that Mrs Budley generously contributed her furniture, for there will be a bed and linen for you, Miss James. But my servants must not spend their declining years in waiting on all of us. I regret to say that we must all help out. I have a few suggestions. We should each keep our rooms clean and neat and carry down our own slops. Betty has told me that, again thanks to Mrs Budley, the drawing room is once more in use. We may retire there this evening, for John has been able to obtain more timber and we may have a fire but only if the evening should prove chilly. Miss James, you said you were good with figures. On the road home, the colonel agreed that you should take over the handling of our accounts. Everything is to be shared equally. If we look like we're running low on supplies, before we start to sell off anything else, perhaps we should each write to our relatives and suggest we are invited on a visit. We each take a large trunk with us and bring back what food or coals we can. Make sure you are not caught taking anything. I have had a recent distressing experience I do not wish to relate at the moment. I assure you I have no intention of suggesting we undergo the indignity of visits to our relations unless we have to.'

'Hear, hear!' cried Miss Tonks, thinking of her sister and then blushing when she found herself the centre of attention.

'I have a suggestion to make,' said Harriet.

'Go on,' said the colonel. 'Let's hear it.'

'I am a very good cook. When my parents were alive, they employed a French chef and he trained me because I asked him to. I can create very good dishes out of next to nothing, and provided Betty does not object to me in her kitchen, I could handle that side of things, including the shopping. I know all the best markets.'

'My dear Miss James,' said Lady Fortescue haughtily, 'there is no need to stoop so low.'

'It is more dignified than carrying down slops,' pointed out Harriet.

'It sounds like fun,' said Mrs Budley with a giggle. 'Miss Tonks and I could help, too.'

'Very well,' said Lady Fortescue grandly. 'Betty will not object.'

Harriet flicked a glance at Betty, whose face registered the well-trained absolutely nothing of the good servant.

'So now that we have had our tea,' said Lady Fortescue, 'Miss James should go with John and collect her things.'

And so the poor relations settled down to what, for them, seemed an idyllic way of life. Mrs Budley had brought her piano and played to them in the evenings while Miss Tonks sang, the spinster having a surprisingly beautiful voice. Harriet produced a 'chicken' casserole and then amazed them all by telling them it was rabbit. They were warm and well fed. Only Harriet, carefully working out the accounts, knew that it could not last much longer.

If they had thought of a saviour, they would all have thought of some knight errant looking rather like the handsome Duke of Rowcester, particularly Harriet, who found she dreamt of him often.

But not one of them would ever have thought of the unlovely person of Sir Philip Sommerville.

Sir Philip was old and smelly and arthritic. He was well connected. He had in the past not waited for rich relatives to invite him but had simply descended on them. Unlike Lady Fortescue, he was an expert thief and always took, not only some little objet d'art that he could sell, but practical things like cheese, ham and bread, and always travelled with an extra large empty trunk for the purpose of filling it up with what he could take from the kitchens of whatever stately home he happened to be in.

But thievery demanded a certain quickness and agility. His shoulders were stooped, and his once beautiful hands knotted and gnarled. His sparse hair clung to his pink scalp and his face looked like that of an elderly tortoise.

He had given up grooming himself or washing

some time ago. Colonel Sandhurst and Lady Fortescue had got downwind of him in Hyde Park, and that had been enough. They had moved on without speaking to him.

But Sir Philip had noticed their close scrutiny and the way they had shaken their heads and his interest was quickened. He scuttled after them and demanded to know why they had been staring at him.

Lady Fortescue raised a scented handkerchief to her nose and from behind its barrier said coldly that if he washed, he might present himself at her home in Bond Street at two on the following afternoon.

Sir Philip stalked off, greatly offended. And yet that spark of curiosity would not go away. What if this Lady Fortescue, as she had introduced herself, were to prove some sort of philanthropist? There might be money in it for him.

So he sold a little silver box he had stolen from a niece. It was a pretty thing used in the early part of the eighteenth century for storing lice. For when you plucked the occasional louse from your clothes, it was only polite to put the thing away in a box rather than offend society by crushing it in public or flicking it onto the floor where it would be free to leap onto someone else. He had been keeping it in reserve. He lived in one room above a butcher's shop in Shepherd Market. Now he took himself off to the Hummuns, the Turkish baths in Jermyn Street, and finally emerged pink and scented. He realized his clothes stank, so he went and bought clean clothes and underclothes with what was left, and also reclaimed his china false teeth from the pawn and substituted them for his second-best set, which was of wood.

Before calling on Bond Street, he went into a perfumer's and asked to try several samples before shaking his head and saying none of them would do. Lady Fortescue opened the door herself to him and nearly fainted as a great wave of scent hit her in the face.

Sir Philip was brought before the others, questioned and then told to wait outside the drawing room while they decided on their verdict. Lady Fortescue said firmly that the man was impossible. But Colonel Sandhurst, whose spirits had come back under the influence of food and warmth, was beginning to resent Lady Fortescue's high-handed manner and so he said he seemed all right to him. The others, who also thought Lady Fortescue took too much upon herself, sided with the colonel.

So Sir Philip came to stay.

And they should all have been happy. They all had what they had craved, food and companionship. It was when Harriet produced the accounts book and said they must do something soon to gain money that the real cracks began to show.

'It's a pity none of you females has been trained to work,' said Sir Philip waspishly. 'I mean, take Miss Tonks there. No good to man nor beast.'

Miss Tonks began to weep, and Harriet coldly told Sir Philip that he had proved himself to be the most worthless member of all, as he never did anything to help. The colonel said sarcastically that he had no doubt Lady Fortescue would tell them all what to do as she usually did, and Lady Fortescue asked him acidly if he would like to go back to his old life and the colonel said huffily it might not be a bad idea, for he was tired of petticoat government, and then everyone relapsed into a bitter silence.

It was broken at last by Harriet. 'The trouble is,' she said firmly, 'that we have not enough to do with our time. If we were proper members of society, then we would be making calls and going to parties and dances and things like that. Or if we were servants, we would not have time to quarrel. Look at the servants at Limmer's Hotel down the street. Limmer's is always crowded from one year's end to the next, for there are just not enough hotels in London.'

Sir Philip looked around and said suddenly, 'This could be a hotel. Lots of room. Make a fortune.'

'Oh, really,' exclaimed Miss Tonks with rare sarcasm. 'And where would we get the money to pay for the alterations? And a chef? All good hotels have a renowned chef.'

'As to that,' said Harriet slowly, 'I could do that.'

'Do you mean that we should stoop to being in trade, that *we* should become hotel servants?' demanded Lady Fortescue.

'Survive the first Season and we'd have money to hire servants,' said Sir Philip. 'But don't you see, all we would have to do would be to get the readies to start the place up, and before you know it all our

30

relations would be on the doorstep, clamouring to buy us out!'

The colonel thought of his rich cousin. He thought of visits to his other relatives, always invited when there were no other guests, snubbed by the servants, patronized . . .

'I'd agree to the scheme,' he said, 'but how do we get the money? If we had the money, we would not be having this discussion.'

Sir Philip leaned forward, his small head poking out of his high collar. 'We don't wait to be invited. I never do. Drop in on the richest of them and stay long enough to steal something valuable.'

There was an outcry against this. Then Lady Fortescue in a shaky voice told them of the stealing of the candlesticks and her subsequent humiliation. The Duke of Rowcester, thought Harriet, remembering his handsome face and grey eyes. Was he married?

But Sir Philip's pale eyes began to gleam. 'You ain't doing it right,' he said to Lady Fortescue. 'A small gold object would've fetched more and not have been missed till you were clear away. You're an amateur. Let a professional do it first.'

'Very well,' said Lady Fortescue frostily. 'You go first. You set an example and prove it's not all talk.'

'Oh, it's not talk. I'll get something if I can which'll start us off. Now, what about a bottle of burgundy to send me on my way?'

What Sir Philip did not tell them was where he meant to go. He was, in fact, like Lady Fortescue, a relative of the Duke of Rowcester, but a very distant one. So distant that he had never been invited to the stately home. He decided it was time he cashed in on it. Besides, under his unlovely exterior and waspish manner, Sir Philip was fond of Lady Fortescue and wanted to enrich them all and at the same time get revenge on the duke for her humiliation.

It was true that the Duke of Rowcester was still accounted handsome, but perhaps now more because of his title and fortune. There was a perpetual frozen haughtiness of manner about him that robbed his looks of any appeal or charm.

He was at his frostiest when his butler told him that his uncle, Sir Philip Sommerville, had arrived.

From his great height, the duke looked down at the small bent man with the china teeth and said awfully, 'I have never heard of you.'

'Don't suppose you have,' said Sir Philip cheerfully. 'I'm several times removed, so to speak.'

With a look that said Sir Philip was not far enough removed, the duke called for the map of the family tree and there, sure enough, albeit out on a twig, was Sir Philip Sommerville.

'Do you plan to stay long?' demanded the duke glacially.

'Only a week,' said Sir Philip.

The duke relaxed. He had expected Sir Philip to say something like six months. 'I am very busy at the moment,' said the duke, 'but ask the servants for anything you need.'

'You are most kind,' said Sir Philip, giving a courtly bow.

The butler led him up to a richly appointed guest chamber. 'Mrs Herriot, the housekeeper, will be with you presently, sir,' he said. 'If there is anything further you wish, you have only to ring. If you wish a bath, his grace has had a bathroom installed.'

Sir Philip scowled, thinking that the butler was suggesting he was a trifle ripe, and certainly he had not had much of a wash since he had joined the poor relations.

'We are most proud of it, sir,' the butler went on. 'We are sure we are one of the few stately homes in England which has a bathroom.'

'I may have a wash shortly,' said Sir Philip. 'Where is it?'

'It is in the basement.'

'What? In the servants' quarters?'

'No, sir. This is an old pile and was built in the seventeenth century. The servants' quarters are in the rustic at the side of the house. The new bathroom is conveniently situated under the hall.'

'Perhaps before dinner,' said Sir Philip, thinking what an odd cove this duke must be to give up any living space to house a bath when the wretched thing could be easily carried up the stairs by the servants. Besides, all this washing, except for medicinal purposes, was deuced odd.

The butler left and was shortly replaced by a buxom housekeeper.

'This is a splendid mansion,' said Sir Philip ingratiatingly.

'Yes, indeed,' beamed the housekeeper.

'I would appreciate a tour of it tomorrow, if you would be so good.'

'Certainly, sir. I would be honoured.'

An hour later, led by a liveried footman, Sir Philip descended to the bathroom. A marble bath was sunk into the floor. Hot water was supplied by an elaborate machine at the head of the bath, a form of oil heater which the footman proceeded to light. Sir Philip watched with interest as the bath slowly filled with steaming water. The footman sprinkled it with rose water, added cold water, tested the temperature with his elbow rather like a mother testing the bath water for the baby, and then helped Sir Philip out of his clothes.

Sir Philip descended a flight of marble steps into the bath and then sank slowly into the water. He thought he could get to like bathing such as this. The great house above him was hushed and quiet. Nothing to disturb him but the sound of scented water lapping against the marble sides. When the water was beginning to get cold, he tugged on a long bell rope which hung over the bath and this time two footmen in oilskin aprons appeared, helped him out and assisted him to dress.

Back in his room, he ordered brandy and then began to look around. There was a good French clock on the mantel, but that would hardly get the builders started on the hotel. Best to wait for the grand tour of the house and see what he could see.

The duke did not join him for dinner that evening, but Sir Philip, eating his way through many delicious courses washed down with first-class wine, did not care. He did not crave the duke's liking, only some of his wealth.

On the following day, he followed Mrs Herriot, the housekeeper, about, asking questions about the family portraits, although he was not interested in any of them. It was when he came to the muniments room that he had an effort to look casual and uninterested. For among the glass cases of family relics, swords and awards and manuscripts was one holding a necklace which sparkled and winked evilly in the dim light of the room. It was a barbaric necklace of heavy gold set with rubies, pearls, diamonds and emeralds, great chunks of stones. With seeming indifference, Sir Philip damned it as 'a heathen, vulgar thing' and Mrs Herriot agreed, saying the late duke had brought it from the East.

'Mind you, the stones are very fine,' said Sir Philip airily. 'I wonder the duke does not fear it might get stolen.'

'Mercy, sir,' said Mrs Herriot, raising her plump hands. 'Who would dare to steal from a duke?'

'I have a strange request,' said Sir Philip, wrenching his eyes away from the glittering gems with an effort, 'I would like to see your kitchens, if that is not too much trouble.'

Mrs Herriot was delighted. Sir Philip spent a whole hour inspecting everything and asking questions, and she was not to know that his eyes had taken in the contents of the well-stocked larder.

Sir Philip did not see the duke that day either, and again he did not care.

He slept lightly and rose at two in the morning. He slipped out of his bedroom and crept up to the attics at the top of the east wing. 'We won't bother going up there,' Mrs Herriot had said. 'The servants sleep in the attics in the west wing, and the ones in the east are used for storing all the old furniture.'

Taking a thin piece of metal from his pocket just in case the doors should prove to be locked, Sir Philip tried the handle of the first door. It turned easily and soon he was inside. He took a candle from his dressing-gown pocket and a flat stand from his other, along with a tinder-box, and soon was holding the candle up to inspect the contents of the attic.

There were great pieces of carved Jacobean furniture, piles of old-fashioned clothes, bits of dinner services, cast-offs of all kinds.

He went from there to the attic room next door. Here he found what he had been hoping to discover, chests full of expensive ladies' gewgaws. He helped himself to three silver patch-boxes, four fans with carved ivory sticks, several gold-topped scent bottles, the gold knob from a broken cane, a small clock which didn't work but had a case of solid gold and the silver top off a long walking-cane.

He found a bag full of sewing silks, emptied it and put his treasures inside. Then he made his way quietly back to his room.

The servants all thought Sir Philip was a very nice old gentleman and that it was a pity the duke did not show more courtesy and respect to his relative. So when Sir Philip said plaintively that he wondered whether it might be possible to borrow a carriage and drive to the nearest town to see the sights, all was quickly arranged, particularly as the thoughtful old gentleman said he would drive himself, and a gig or any other light carriage would suffice.

The nearest town of Ledcham, he was told, was only six miles away.

Taking his haul of stolen goods with him, he set off in a gig pulled by a glossy pony.

At Ledcham, he stabled the pony at an inn in the centre and then began to search the backstreets until his nose for villainy told him he had found the right sort of jeweller. He haggled away over the sale of the goods and then said he would settle for a lower figure if the jeweller would take more from him on the morrow, to which the greedy jeweller agreed. Sir Philip then bought a drawing-pad, pencils and paints and returned to the duke's, feeling satisfied with himself.

The duke eventually came across Sir Philip, who was sketching the hall. 'Why, that is very good, sir,' said the duke in surprise. 'You are indeed an accomplished artist.'

'You have a beautiful home. I thought I would make some sketches of it,' said Sir Philip, and returned to his work. By evening, and after a pleasant dinner with the duke which did not trouble Sir Philip's conscience one bit, he had made a sketch of that necklace down to the last detail.

For the rest of the week, Sir Philip raided during the night and sold the stuff during the day, so that by the end of his stay he was able to tip the butler and housekeeper handsomely, so that when they subsequently found a surprising amount of stuff missing from the larder, they blamed a housemaid who had left the week before.

Sir Philip, who had arrived in a hired hack after taking the stage to Ledcham, returned in the duke's travelling carriage with a trunkful of all the goods he had stolen from the larder on his last night.

He decided not to tell the others of his plan in detail, or where he had been. Lady Fortescue, he was sure, would go white at the idea of the duke's being robbed and think that just because she had been caught out, he would be found out as well.

So he said he was about to take something extraordinarily valuable from a relative of his, that he had a sketch of it, that he had raised enough money to get it copied. All he had to do was leave the substitute and the fake would probably never be discovered. Sir Philip did not care whether it was, but he did not tell them that. For by the time the duke noticed, he was sure there would have been plenty of other people staying in the house.

The others were not surprised that Sir Philip knew some villain who would do the craftsmanship. As in the eighteenth century, when Sir Philip had been a young man, the minor lights of society and a few of the major ones drifted between the salons of the great and the villainous dives of London. Sir Philip found the man to craft the fake necklace, he paid him and, when it was ready, set out so that he would arrive at the duke's during the night.

He let himself in by a terrace window which he had already noticed had a lock that was easy to pick. He had memorized the geography of the house and so was able to move quietly in the dark.

With a special little pick, he unlocked the case, lifted the necklace out and put it in his pocket and carefully arranged the substitute, glad that bright moonlight was shining into the room and he did not have to risk lighting a candle.

The deed was done.

It was only when he was returning to London that he suddenly realized he had a fortune in his pocket. Why not sell it and keep the money for himself? He could live like a gentleman once more. He deserved a reward. He had never stolen anything so valuable before, never committed such an elaborately plotted crime.

But somehow, since he knew he was not much liked, the thought of the sheer loneliness of that old life made him go straight back to Bond Street, open the door of the drawing room and cry out, 'Order the builders. We are going into business!'

THREE

Let not ambition mock their useful toil,
Their homely joys and destiny obscure;
Nor grandeur hear with a disdainful smile
The short and simple annals of the poor.

THOMAS GRAY

The fashionable hotels were The Clarendon, Limmer's, Ibbetson's, Fladong's, Stephen's and Grillon's. The Clarendon was kept by a French cook, Jacquiers, and was the only public hotel that served a genuine French dinner, for which you seldom paid less than three or four pounds, with a bottle of claret or champagne costing a guinea.

Limmer's was in Bond Street and an evening resort for the sporting world. As the famous Regency diarist Captain Gronow put it, '. . . in fact it was a midnight Tattersall's, where you heard nothing but the language of the turf, and where men with not very clean hands used to make up their books.' Limmer's was rated as the dirtiest hotel in London, but in its gloomy, comfortless coffee room might be seen many members of the rich squirearchy who visited London during the sporting season. This hotel was so crowded that quite often a bed could not be obtained for any amount of money, but they served a good, plain English dinner and their gin punch, named after their waiter, Tom Collins, was famous.

Ibbetson's Hotel was chiefly patronized by the clergy and by young men from the universities. The charges there were not very high. Fladong's in Oxford Street was the haunt of naval men, for there was no club for sailors. Stephen's, like Limmer's, was also in Bond Street, and used by army officers and men about town. If any stranger without the right social credentials asked to dine there, he was stared at by the servants and assured that there was no table available. The menu was simple: boiled fish and joints of meat.

These then formed the competition for the new hotel taking shape inside the discreet frontage of Lady Fortescue's home. Despite the fact that the poor relations had to make their quarters in the attics, there were hardly ever any outbursts of temper. Miss Tonks, terrified at first by the enormity of the risk they were taking, and by her future as a hotel servant, had gradually blossomed in the odd company in which she found herself and had recently roused herself to call Sir Philip a 'malevolent old pig', to cheers from everyone but Sir Philip, who looked as surprised as if a pet lapdog had savaged him. Not that Sir Philip and his horrible china teeth, which he had a nasty habit of leaving about the place, was often with them.

The old man had apparently forgotten that the main reason for the hotel was to provoke their relatives to buy them out. He seemed consumed with ambition to make the hotel the best in London and even overrode Lady Fortescue's objections that too much gold paint was being used in the hall.

'Dazzle 'em on entrance,' said Sir Philip. 'Mirrors and gilt and thick carpet. Put a thin red one over a lot of felt. Demme, I would give my back teeth for a chandelier.'

'You already have given your back teeth,' said Lady Fortescue waspishly, but Sir Philip was off and preparing for another raiding visit on his relatives.

This time he chose his nephew, Mr Tommy Brickhampton, although with a certain reluctance. He was fond of Tommy, even though he knew that Mrs Tommy dreaded his visits.

True to form, he turned up unannounced just as the fashionable Mrs Tommy was giving a house party. Sir Philip had behaved badly in the past, but this time even his nephew considered that Sir Philip was going out of his way to be particularly obnoxious. His table manners were worse than ever and he appeared to delight in insulting the guests, especially the ladies.

Driven by his anguished wife, after the fourth day of this social hell, Tommy took his uncle aside and said he would really have to go.

To his alarm, Sir Philip began to cry, or that is what it looked like, Sir Philip having scrubbed his eyes with a raw onion hidden in his handkerchief.

'I am so sorry,' said Sir Philip, giving all the appearance of a pathetically broken old man. 'I lead such a dull and lonely life. I am not used to company. Before I take myself off, could I ask you for a little present?'

'Anything,' said Tommy awkwardly, beginning to privately damn his poor wife as a heartless fiend.

'You know how I poke around the place?' said Sir Philip.

'Oh, yes,' said Tommy with feeling.

'In that saloon in the west wing, the one you never use . . .'

'We will be using it,' said Tommy quickly. 'Getting the builders in. Wall's a bit shaky.'

'There is a chandelier there I would love. With something glittering and beautiful like that to light my old age, I would die happy.'

'But that's Waterford crystal!'

'Oh, well, I feared it was too much to ask. When's dinner?'

'Look, Unk,' said Tommy, 'I don't want to appear heartless or crude, but I'll strike a bargain with you. I'll give you that chandelier if you promise not to visit us for a year.'

Sir Philip debated whether he ought to cry again, but the onion had made his eyes sore, and so he said, 'Very well, my boy. And if I could have your travelling carriage to take it back to London . . . ?'

'Yes, yes, but if you could leave quickly. I mean to say, no reason for long-drawn-out leave-takings, hey?'

And so Sir Philip and the enormous chandelier wrapped in a Holland cloth were loaded into the travelling carriage while Mrs Tommy stood and watched balefully, clasping and unclasping her little hands and muttering to her husband, 'How could you? That was a wedding present from Lord Frame!'

Even Lady Fortescue had to admit that, once it was hung in the hall, the chandelier looked magnificent.

The old schoolroom up among the attics was their dining room and drawing room combined. They were relaxing after one of Harriet's excellent dinners when Mrs Budley put down a piece of sewing she had been working on and said, 'What is the hotel to be called?'

'The Palace,' suggested the colonel.

'Too vulgar by half,' said Lady Fortescue. 'We should call it Fortescue's Hotel.'

'What about an acronym, using our names?' said Miss Tonks.

Harriet wrote it down. 'That comes to JTBFSS; can't get a word out of that.'

'I have it,' said Sir Philip. 'The Poor Relation.'

'What!'

'Think on't. That'll get the relatives coming in droves. And look at it this way. It suggests cachet, economy and the sort of name that only anyone very aristocratic would dare to call a place. All those other hotels are really just extensions of men's clubs. But what about a hotel where the ladies could stay for the Season, families could stay? We could charge the earth and they would pay, because it would spare them the price of a rented town house, the price of servants and the price of food.'

'It's outrageous. But you might have something there,' said the colonel slowly. He looked down at his sparkling new Hessian boots for comfort. It had been Harriet who had suggested they each buy something they wanted very much before the builders started work. She herself had bought a delicate little fan, a useless trifle to remind her of elegant, carefree days long gone. Lady Fortescue had bought a gilt fob-watch, the one that she had given to the pawn having been sold by the pawnbroker long ago. Miss Tonks had bought a lace collar; Mrs Budley a bonnet and Sir Philip a large bottle of scent.

'I think I like it,' said Miss Tonks.

'Oh, now that the spinster has given it her blessing,' jeered Sir Philip, 'we have nothing to worry about.'

'I think you are the most unlovable creature I have ever come across,' said Miss Tonks hotly.

Harriet looked across at her in affectionate amusement. No longer the thin, dithering, faded woman she had been, Miss Tonks was gaining colour and character.

'Don't let's quarrel,' pleaded Mrs Budley. 'I can't bear it.'

Mrs Budley had just surprised them all by selling all her pretty clothes and keeping only the plain, serviceable ones.

'Now then, m'dear,' said the colonel gallantly. 'No one wants to upset *you*.'

'No, indeed,' agreed Lady Fortescue, but she was suddenly seized with an uncharacteristic fit of jealousy at the sight of the colonel smiling on the widow.

'That's it, then,' said Sir Philip. 'The Poor Relation it is!'

By the following January, the sign was hoisted high over the building. Advertisements in the newspapers described the new venture as 'a discreet hotel for families attending the London Season'.

Little crowds gathered outside, peering in at the dazzling hall and that glittering chandelier. In country houses the length and breadth of England, the new hotel was discussed.

'Oh, dear,' said Mr Tommy. 'There's a big piece in the *Morning Post* about this new hotel, The Poor Relation.'

'What an odd name,' exclaimed his wife.

'It's worse than that. It's being run by six people.'

'Who are they? Some of those French people, I suppose.'

'The names of the owners are listed as Lady Fortescue, Colonel Sandhurst, Miss Letitia Tonks, Miss Harriet James, Mrs Eliza Budley and . . . Sir Philip Sommerville.'

'The old wretch,' said his wife bitterly. 'He has done this out of spite. Poor relation, indeed!'

'Can't have this,' said Tommy miserably. 'Think

of the shame on the family. Better go and see if we can buy him out.'

A steely look appeared in his wife's beautiful eyes. 'On the contrary,' she said evenly, 'it gives us a good excuse to have nothing to do with the old horror again.'

Honoria, Mrs Blessop, stared at the newspaper as if she could not believe her eyes. But the Letitia Tonks mentioned could not be her sister. Letitia had very little money, and certainly not enough to be a partner in a hotel. Still, it would perhaps be wise to call when she was in London for the Season. And if it should prove to be her sister, she would drag her out of there by the hair.

The Duke of Rowcester read the article several times. He did not care what Sir Philip did. The man was nothing to him. But Lady Fortescue. She must be really mad. And that other name, Harriet James. But it could not be *his* Harriet, not that startling beauty who had intrigued him so long ago. But it was his duty to protect his family name and stop Lady Fortescue in this obviously senile folly.

In a great dreary pile on the Yorkshire moors, Lady Bunbary, proud mother of two plain daughters, read the article very carefully. She had already rented a house for the Season at a great price. This hotel had very high charges. On the other hand, it would save the expense of moving the servants to London, not

47

to mention the cost of that town house. She put the matter to her husband, who as usual said, 'You must do as you feel fit, my dear.' And so she sat down at her writing desk and cancelled the hire of the town house and then wrote another letter to The Poor Relation booking rooms for the Season for herself, her husband, her two daughters, her maid and her husband's valet. And so The Poor Relation got its first customers.

More bookings followed, and by the first day of the Season, the hotel was full. Not only was the hotel full, but society fought to try to get bookings for dinner, for the food was reported to be superb, and then there was the novelty of being served at dinner by old Lady Fortescue and Colonel Sandhurst.

In competition with Limmer's famous Tom Collins, named after the clever waiter who had invented the cocktail, Sir Philip had come up with the Sommerville Blast, a mixture of rum, arrack, gin, honey, herbs and soda water.

Harriet had engaged other servants, but Sir Philip made sure that the six of them were always in view, doing menial jobs. That was what added to the cachet, and as the hotel prospered so, the poor relations found that a great deal of the work was being done for them by an increasing army of servants . . . with the exception of Harriet.

She worked wonders in the kitchen to keep the cooking budget low, knowing that they must show a large profit by the end of the Season. But she was proud of the hotel and her part in the running of it.

She only wished Sir Philip would stop his tricks, would stop cheating the guests.

Lady Bunbary sat down on a pretty gilt chair in her room the day she arrived and it broke under her. Sir Philip tut-tutted and added the price of a new chair to her bill without a conscience, although he had sawn through most of the legs so that just such an accident would happen. He gleefully took away the remains of the chair, glued it together and put it in someone else's room to await another profitable accident. He broke handles off water jugs and glued them on lightly so that when they, too, broke, the guest could be charged for the damage, and so a small hoard of cunningly broken objects found their way from bedchamber to bedchamber.

Harriet slaved away over her cooking pots, only occasionally mounting the area steps to take the air and look wistfully at the young misses leaving the hotel for some social engagement, chattering and carefree, sending clouds of scent down Bond Street.

She wondered sometimes if her life had really changed for the better or whether she had not sentenced herself to perpetual drudgery.

One evening when she was enjoying a brief rest at the top of the area steps, a splendid carriage pulled by four white horses rolled to a stop in front of The Poor Relation. The coach panels were crested and there was a magnificent coachman on the box as well as outriders. Two footmen jumped down from the back-strap and lifted down the steps. Strange; it was rather like that magnificent coach which had brought back Sir Philip from his first raiding expedition, although the old man had steadfastly refused to say where he had been.

A tall man alighted from the coach and stood looking up at the front of the hotel. Harriet shrank back. It was the Duke of Rowcester. He looked grimmer and more austere than she remembered.

She darted down the area steps and shot up to the little office off the hall, where she found Lady Fortescue, Sir Philip and Colonel Sandhurst gleefully poring over the books.

'The Duke of Rowcester has arrived,' gasped Harriet.

'Dear me,' said Lady Fortescue. 'Now the trouble begins.'

'I would be glad, so very glad,' said Harriet in a rush, 'if you did not tell him about me. I mean, my name has been in the newspapers, but you could say *that* Harriet James is a sleeping partner and . . . and . . . quite an old lady. I knew him once and I would not like him to discover I am working as a cook.'

Lady Fortescue squared her shoulders. 'Have no fear. He will be so angry with me, he will not be interested in anyone else. Why are you looking so shifty, Sir Philip? It is not as if he is your relative. Your arm, Colonel. Let us face the enemy together.'

Lady Fortescue leaned quite heavily on the colonel's arm so that he forgot he had often damned her as an unfeminine, bossy old trout and felt a wave of protectiveness as they walked into the hall and faced the Duke of Rowcester.

'Madam,' said the duke coldly, removing his hat to reveal a head of thick golden hair, 'is there somewhere we may be private?'

Lady Fortescue inclined her head. 'But Colonel Sandhurst comes with me,' she said. 'There is nothing that need be kept private from him.'

He bowed in assent and she led the way back to the office. Sir Philip looked up as they entered and blushed, for, perhaps, the first time in his life. 'Well, well,' said the duke nastily, 'another relative. Dear me, Colonel Sandhurst, you are not perhaps related to me as well?'

Lady Fortescue's hand trembled slightly on the colonel's arm. 'We were not aware Sir Philip was related to you.'

'Nor was I,' said the duke, 'until he descended on me last year.'

Lady Fortescue and the colonel exchanged startled glances as it dawned on them both at the same time that the Duke of Rowcester was probably that mysterious relative from whom Sir Philip had stolen something of tremendously high value. Shades of the prison house passed before Lady Fortescue's eyes and she said weakly, 'I must sit down.'

'Leave you all to it,' said Sir Philip cheerfully, cheerful because the duke had obviously not noticed that necklace was a fake, and he scurried off.

Lady Fortescue sat down behind a small ornate desk, the colonel stood behind her with one hand on her shoulder, and the duke faced them both.

'You have shamed our family,' said the duke.

'On the contrary,' said Lady Fortescue, suddenly rallying, 'I have brought credit to the family by being part of a successful business.'

'By going into *trade*?'

'I am quite decided there is nothing dishonourable in trade,' said Lady Fortescue firmly.

'I will not refer in front of this gentleman to your unfortunate behaviour on your last visit to me,' said the duke icily, 'but that, combined with this, persuades me that I have sufficient grounds to have you committed to the nearest madhouse.'

Lady Fortescue trembled under the grip of the colonel's reassuring hand, which tightened as he said, 'Come, your grace, Lady Fortescue has all her wits, and besides, she cannot be committed if her husband says she is sane.'

'Her husband, Colonel Sandhurst, has been dead these past twenty years.'

'Perhaps I should explain myself better, your grace. Lady Fortescue is affianced to me.'

Lady Fortescue's black eyes went quite blank, but she did not utter a word.

The duke's temper rose even higher. This elderly couple, both dressed in formal black, were making him feel somehow shabby.

'Take warning,' he said, addressing himself to Lady Fortescue, 'I have great social power. I will have you closed down any way I can.'

He turned and left abruptly.

'I do not know how to thank you, Colonel,' said Lady Fortescue warmly.

He laughed. 'Oh, I don't mind telling the odd lie from time to time.'

And for some reason Lady Fortescue felt bitterly depressed.

The duke meanwhile marched into the hall and looked about him. His cold eyes fell on Sir Philip, who was slowly retreating backwards as if trying to escape unnoticed.

'Ah, Sir Philip,' said the duke, 'I have a mind to stay here.'

'Unfortunately,' said Sir Philip, 'we are fully booked.'

'Let me see the register.'

Sir Philip led him to a small desk which held a heavy leather-bound ledger, which he opened. The duke ran his eyes down the names.

'I see Bunbary is down from Yorkshire. Have my card sent up.'

Sir Philip snapped his arthritic fingers and handed the duke's card to a small page and told the boy to take it up to Lord Bunbary.

The duke waited patiently until the boy returned and said that Lord and Lady Bunbary would be pleased to receive him.

Sir Philip waited a few moments and then scuttled up to the Bunbarys' suite, which was on the first floor, and put his ear to the door.

'Call it a whim,' he heard the duke saying, 'but I have an idea I would like to stay here. As there is no room to be had, I suggest offering you the use of my town house and servants in exchange.'

Sir Philip gloomily heard the Bunbarys' effusive thanks before he crept away to break the news to the others.

The duke, no sooner had he installed himself and his valet, proceeded to examine the contents of his sitting room and bedroom with a quizzing-glass. He noticed the carefully glued handles on the vases, the water jugs and even the chamber-pot. He also noticed that the legs of one of the chairs looked suspicious. He had stayed in many hotels in his youth while making the Grand Tour with an amusing and worldly tutor who had briefed him on all the tricks of rapacious hoteliers. He rang the bell and told Sir Philip, who answered its summons, to take away all the damaged stuff, which his valet had arranged in the middle of the sitting-room floor.

'Goodness,' said Sir Philip, quite unrepentant, 'what a set of vandals those Bunbarys turned out to be. I must send them a bill.'

'You will not send them a bill, you old thief,' said the duke acidly. 'If I search your room, I will no doubt find an interesting array of objects cleverly damaged for the purpose of milking more money from your guests.'

'I do not know why you stay here,' said Sir Philip plaintively. 'Your town house would be much more comfortable.'

'I am staying here to get adequate proof that Lady Fortescue is demented.'

'And would you enjoy that?' asked Sir Philip

curiously. 'Would you enjoy dragging an old lady out of the comfort of a well-run hotel and putting her in a madhouse? Would you enjoy her terror, her tears?'

'Do not be sentimental,' said the duke coldly. 'If a woman of Lady Fortescue's breeding and lineage stoops to trade, then there is something up with her wits. I shall not put her in a madhouse. I shall see that she and her future husband are cared for in a manner that befits their station.'

Wrinkles of sheer surprise ran up Sir Philip's forehead and across his balding scalp like ripples fleeing from a stone dropped in a pond.

He abstractedly picked up a chamber-pot from the floor. The handle fell off and the rest of it rolled off into a corner, but he stood dazed, staring at the duke, holding the broken handle in his hand. 'Her *what?*' he eventually asked.

'Colonel Sandhurst tells me they are to be married.'

'Ho, they are, are they?' demanded Sir Philip, suddenly and furiously. 'I'll have a few words to say about that. Sneaking off behind my back.'

'Stop making a cake of yourself, Sir Philip. You are not in your teens. You are all about one hundred and two. The idea of anyone of Lady Fortescue's age contemplating marriage is ridiculous.'

'What would you know about it, you young whipper-snapper?' demanded Sir Philip.

'Remember to whom you speak, Sir Philip. I am not in the way of tolerating insolence.'

'Then find somewhere else to live, you chisel-faced twat,' shouted Sir Philip and stormed out. Then he opened the door again and hurled the broken handle of the chamber-pot at the duke and crashed out again.

The duke walked over to the fireplace and pulled the bell rope. After a few moments, the door opened and Miss Tonks came in.

'You rang, your grace?'

'I asked Sir Philip to remove' – he pointed a finger at the glued objects in the middle of the floor – 'this garbage. Instead of doing so, he subjected me to a deal of insolence.'

'But he is always insolent,' said Miss Tonks in mild surprise. 'I will have the items collected directly and replaced with new. I hope everything else is to your satisfaction, your grace.'

He studied her thoughtfully. She was an obvious spinster, of middle height, with faded brown hair and a faded face. But there was breeding in her long nose, long thin hands and long thin feet, and in the slightly mangled use of her vowels, which all ladies attained after a lifetime of being told to mind their Prunes and Prisms, that is, never to stretch the lips when enunciating any word.

'Are you a partner in this establishment?' he asked.

'Yes, your grace, Miss Tonks at your service.'

'You amaze me.'

A year ago Miss Tonks would have stammered ad blushed, but had she not trounced the vile Sir

Philip on numerous occasions? 'If you mean, your grace, that it is odd to find a lady working as a servant, I consider that a highly flattering observation.'

'Why?'

'Having gone into trade, your grace, I considered I had left the days of being ladylike behind.'

He felt his anger subsiding before her mild gaze. After all, his quarrel was with Lady Fortescue, not her.

He turned and walked up and down the room. His legs, thought Miss Tonks, were really excellent, and probably all his own. He did not look like the sort of man to wear padded calves. His waist was slim and his hips narrow, his shoulders in a well-tailored coat were broad and owed nothing to buckram wadding, of that she was sure. It was an age in which even a spinster assessed the finer points of a man's physique with as sharp an eye as a horse trader at Tattersall's looking at a stallion.

He swung round. 'Miss Tonks, among the list of partners, there is a certain Miss Harriet James.'

'Indeed, yes, your grace,' said Miss Tonks, who had been well coached. 'Such a dear old lady.'

'Old?'

'Oh, yes. Very, very, very old; bedridden, in fact. And deaf and blind,' added Miss Tonks.

'So how is it a blind and deaf and very old lady can still summon up enough strength to interest herself in the founding of a new hotel?'

'That is a question I have often asked myself,'

sighed Miss Tonks. 'But her powers are quite remarkable.'

Sir Philip waited until dinner was over that evening and then pounced on Lady Fortescue as she was crossing the hall and dragged her into the office.

'Behave yourself,' said Lady Fortescue, jerking her arm free.

'What do you think – you're about to get engaged to Colonel Sandhurst without telling me?' raged Sir Philip.

'The only reason that came about,' said Lady Fortescue evenly, two patches of colour burning on her white cheeks, 'is because the Duke of Rowcester declared his intention of proving me insane and having me committed to a madhouse. Colonel Sandhurst gallantly stepped in and said he was affianced to me only to protect me, that is all. But what concern is it of yours?'

Sir Philip eyed the thin, erect figure of Lady Fortescue, elegant in a severe gown of heavy black silk, the silver-white hair elaborately coiffed under a delicate cap of fine white lace, and the austere white face with its high arched nose and thin scarlet-painted mouth. He clacked his china teeth and leered horribly. 'Just that if you've got any fancies in the direction of love, think of me.' He darted forward and kissed her cheek and then ran out of the room, cackling horribly.

Lady Fortescue raised a hand to her cheek. 'Dear me,' she said, and then she began to giggle like a schoolgirl.

FOUR

By the living jingo, she was all of a muck of sweat.

OLIVER GOLDSMITH

That the great Duke of Rowcester had taken up residence in The Poor Relation was in the newspapers the following morning. Sir Philip had seen to that. He had also advertised that tea and cakes would be served 'with all decorum' to ladies visiting the coffee room. Hopeful mothers and their daughters were soon battling to get in – for was not the duke unmarried?

Down in the kitchen, Harriet was whipping up batch after batch of cakes and wondering when the rush would ever cease so that she could begin preparations for dinner. She had a woman to help with the plain cooking, two scullery maids and a pot-boy, and all of them worked flat out while the heat from the kitchen fire 'roasted them all to a turn', as Harriet's assistant cook, Mrs Bodge, put it. Lady Fortescue's personal servants, Betty and John, had been semi-retired in that their sole job now was to perform light duties in attending to the poor relations in the attics.

59

Harriet finally sent word upstairs that any further cakes would need to be bought.

Then she set about preparing her special 'chicken' dish for dinner, the chicken being rabbit.

Upstairs the duke was furious to find that his very presence was adding to the cachet of The Poor Relation. He had had a busy day, attending to settling the Bunbarys in his town house, visiting old friends and calling on his man of business in the City, but he felt he could not relax until he had done serious damage to the reputation of the hotel. Only, he was persuaded, if the hotel collapsed could he then talk some sense into Lady Fortescue's addled wits.

The Poor Relation did not run to private dining parlours, and so he was forced to descend to the public dining room. He nodded to various society members he knew and took his seat at a table reserved for him which, he noticed bitterly, was in the very centre of the dining room. Sir Philip was determined to turn the duke's stay to their advantage.

The soup and fish courses were faultless, and he could not bring himself to manufacture complaints. But when he tackled the 'chicken' and found a rabbit bone in it, despite Harriet's careful filleting, he decided his moment had come. He stood up and stared awfully about him.

'Rabbit,' he said clearly. The buzz of talk died away.

'I beg your pardon?' Colonel Sandhurst walked up to him.

'This so-called chicken dish is made from rabbit,' said the duke loudly. 'A cheap and shoddy trick.'

'Our French chef is of the finest,' said the colonel in a low voice, hoping to quieten the duke.

'French, hey?' said the duke. 'I shall see this fellow for myself.'

He marched out of the dining room, carefully avoiding Sir Philip's foot, which the old man had stuck out in the hope of tripping the duke up. 'You must not . . .' came the anguished voice of Lady Fortescue after him. 'You cannot . . .'

Unheeding, he strode to the baize door that led to the belowstairs. Huddled together for comfort, Sir Philip, Lady Fortescue and Colonel Sandhurst watched him go, too old to stop him.

At the bottom of the stairs the duke thrust open the kitchen door. A wall of heat struck him.

Mrs Bodge let out a squawk at the sight of the tall man framed in the doorway. He was magnificent in full evening dress, with diamonds sparkling on his long white hands and on the buckles of his shoes. The two scullery maids scurried off to the sink with a pile of dirty dishes. The pot-boy stared open-mouthed.

Harriet had been stooped over the pots hanging above the fire when he entered. She sensed that something had happened, that someone was there who should not be, and turned slowly around and straightened up.

Rivulets of sweat were running down her face and her dress was sticking to her body. Her eyes were very green, enormous in her white face. Her white cap was askew and one long ringlet of glossy black hair hung down on her shoulder.

And yet the duke recognized her. 'Miss James,' he said faintly, 'I came to see the chef.'

'I am the chef,' said Harriet, striving for composure.

'I see . . . I see you are occupied. I shall return after dinner if I may,' he said. He gave a stiff bow and walked out.

He returned to the dining room and sat down again. There was an edgy silence. The other diners studied him nervously.

'I made a mistake,' said the duke, picking up his knife and fork. 'What excellent chicken!'

And the Honourable Mrs Feathers, who had just been saying, before the duke walked in, that she knew it was rabbit because rabbit did not agree with her delicate digestion, suddenly decided it was chicken after all. Everyone began chatting and laughing again. Lady Fortescue felt quite limp with relief.

'Something to do with our Miss James, I think,' said Sir Philip. 'Shocked him into good behaviour.'

'I'll shock him right out of this hotel, see if I don't,' muttered the colonel.

Harriet was too busy at first, arranging the huge dish of floating-island pudding – to be carried upstairs by one of the waiters, who would then dish it out onto assorted plates so that the colonel and Lady Fortescue would only have to hand them round the various tables – to think too much about the duke's unexpected appearance. But once everything had been served and the dishes washed and stacked away and her small staff sent home, for there was no room for them to sleep in the hotel, she sat down wearily at the kitchen table and pulled off her cap and wiped her sweating face. The fire had been banked down for the night. But in the morning, it would need to be stoked up again to cope with all the dishes for breakfast.

She poured herself a glass of wine from a decanter on the table. She was not worried that the duke would return. He had not come to see her, for he had looked nonplussed at the very sight of her. And he had immediately recognized her, as she had recognized him. And yet he *had* changed. There had been no softness or warmth in that hard, proud face. She remembered, wistfully, the laughter in his grey eyes when he had danced with her, and wondered what had happened in the intervening years to make him so cold and proud.

She was sorry he had seen her, for it was the end of a dream that had kept her warm during the sad times of poverty. Sometimes she had even let her fantasies run wild and imagined him finding her one day in the Park and going down on one knee and begging her to be his bride. But the great Duke of Rowcester had no need to beg any woman for anything. He was too sought after. She had learned that he was not yet married, and wondered why.

She should rouse her weary bones and climb up

to the schoolroom and join the others. But she sat on, sipping her wine and wondering if she had strength enough to cope with another day. She should go and tell Sir Philip that no more teas were to be offered. She had enough to do. The servants would have left for the evening, apart from the night staff. None of them lived in. The servants' and owners' dinners were served to them before the diners upstairs. Of course, one of the bells might soon jangle because some guest had decided on a late-night snack. The wires had been arranged so that the bells rang in the school-room as well as the kitchen. Still, tonight was the first of Almack's assemblies and the famous rooms would be crammed with all the members of society lucky enough to have vouchers, so that practically all the hotel guests would be out until the small hours. This of course meant that many of them expected breakfast at two in the afternoon, but then there were always the early birds who wanted steak and beer or kedgeree and tea before a ride in the Park.

Her eyelids began to droop. The kitchen door swung open. Harriet looked up, expecting to see either Miss Tonks or Mrs Budley, for one of them usually came down to the kitchen to talk to her if she did not appear in the schoolroom. The kitchen was now lit only by one candle placed in front of her. But it was the Duke of Rowcester who stood there, his jewels sparkling and dancing in the flickering light of the candle.

Harriet did not feel frightened or ashamed. She only felt very weary.

She stood up and curtsied, and then sat down again and refilled her glass with wine and said in a level voice, 'I trust you have not lost your way, your grace.'

He pulled out a chair and sat down opposite her.

'I have not lost my way, Miss James, but it would appear that you have. What on earth are you doing working like a scullion?'

'I am a partner in this hotel, and its much-admired chef,' said Harriet. 'Wine, your grace?'

'If you please.'

She rose with heartbreaking weariness in every line of her slim body and fetched a clean wineglass and filled it for him before sinking back into her chair.

'Your health, Miss James,' he said, raising his glass. She nodded.

He took a sip of wine and put his glass down on the table.

'I may as well tell you, Miss James, that I am bent on trying to get this folly of a hotel closed down.'

'Why?'

'Is it necessary to explain why? Lady Fortescue is my aunt. She has brought shame on the family. I am convinced she is senile, else she would not have indulged in such a scheme and in such company – saving your presence, Miss James.'

'Lady Fortescue has the sharpest brains of anyone I know,' said Harriet, still in a calm, even voice. 'You cannot call someone mad because she happens to be a partner in a thriving business concern.'

'Then I shall tell you something in confidence. Lady Fortescue is guilty of theft. She attempted to steal two candlesticks from me. And what, may I ask, is a young lady of your undoubted breeding doing here?'

A wave of anger rose up, bringing hot colour to Harriet's white cheeks.

She grasped the edge of the table and glared at him.

'Did you ever ask yourself why this place is called The Poor Relation?'

'Some joke in bad taste, no doubt.'

'We are all – all we partners – poor relations, that most despised class, hoping for crumbs of charity. Had it not been for Lady Fortescue, then my lot would be to live a dreary, impoverished life for the rest of my days. Do you know what it is to be hungry, to be cold in the winter because you cannot afford coals? Why do you think Lady Fortescue stole from you? Madness? Pah! She was *hungry*, your grace, if you can get that simple notion lodged somewhere in that well-coiffed cock-loft of yours. Hungry! That is how she and Colonel Sandhurst met. He *fainted* with hunger in Hyde Park. They found that if we poor relations banded together, we could live better as a group than we could on our own. Sir Philip suggested the hotel.'

'And how did Sir Philip get the money for the building alterations and the furniture?'

Harriet studied her wineglass as if it were the most interesting thing she had ever seen. She was sure, as were the others, that Sir Philip had stolen something of great value from the duke himself. 'He was left a legacy,' she lied, 'and instead of spending it on himself, he decided to help all of us.'

The duke stared at her in silence. He noticed the blue bruises of fatigue under her eyes. The kitchen was cooling down, but he could not forget the furnace heat of earlier.

'Why?' he said at last. 'Why did you not explain your plight to your relations?'

'What good would that do?' she demanded scornfully. 'They know what we get and consider it sufficient.'

'I was not aware that Lady Fortescue was living on so little,' he said. 'But you, you should not be condemned to work down here. Why you? The others make shift to appear to work, but most of it is done by the real servants.'

A cynical gleam appeared in her green eyes. 'At the moment it would cost too much to hire a chef of my calibre. The aristocracy such as we have here do not pay bills in advance. No, that would be too, too vulgar. They pay at the end of their stay, and in some cases we shall be hard put to get them to pay even then. It is a point of honour not to pay tradespeople until the last minute. A professional chef would be too high and mighty to use the cheap ingredients that I do. Because we are an evident success, the grocers, butchers and wine merchants supply us on credit, but soon they will want some of their money.' She passed a hand wearily over her forehead. 'By next year, if all holds good, we shall have a chef and I shall be a lady of comparative leisure.'

'If you live that long,' he remarked. He looked at the open fire. 'Hearth deaths claim many lives each year. Sir Philip's bounty should have stretched to a closed stove.'

She laughed, and he caught his breath as her beauty suddenly blazed out in the gloomy kitchen. 'Ah, you have the right of it,' she said. 'Other women dream of diamonds and rubies from Rundell and Bridge or Mr Hamlit, and I dream of a closed stove.'

'But how did you become so . . . so . . . ?'

'Poor? My parents are both dead. I was left with debts. The usual story. But what of Lady Fortescue now, your grace? I have told you of her sad predicament, so sad it led her to stoop to theft, and yet you appear unmoved.'

'I am not unmoved. I wish she had chosen to explain matters to me instead of venturing on this hotel. I must buy her out.'

And that was what Sir Philip had planned, thought Harriet. But what of the rest of us? 'You might find it difficult,' she said slowly. 'She has found companionship and independence. Why not leave things as they are at present? Everyone has an eccentric in the family. There is no need for you to continue to stay here, even to recognize your aunt. Why, people these days will cut their mothers and fathers in the street if they think them not fashionable enough. I was passing the time in the Park one day last year and I recognized a certain Mr Southern from my brief days in society. He was with a party of dandies from White's. An elderly gentleman nodded to him and his friends asked, "Who was that old man who hailed you in that familiar way?" And Mr Southern replied calmly, "One of my tenant farmers. Splendid chap." But the old man sat down next to me on the bench when they had gone and he burst out that Southern was his *son*.'

'You malign me. I am not thus. But you should not be here. You should be enjoying balls and parties.'

'The only reason, even for a female of my advanced years, to enjoy parties is to find a husband, but believe me, a servant's life gives one a jaded view of the gentlemen of society.'

'How so?'

'We had a typical example of a Bond Street Lounger here just before you came. He strolled into the coffee room with shreds of fabric on his spurs to show he had been "cracking the muslin", or deliberately catching his spurs in the skirts of some poor female in Bond Street. He found fault with every single thing. He damned the waiter and would never let the poor fellow stand still for one moment just to remind him that he was only a servant, a wretched subordinate, and therefore devoid of finer feelings, the idea being that the greater the abuse from him, the greater the waiter was supposed to think his superior qualities. In the dining room, he swore at the fish and said it was not warmed through and the poultry was "as tough as your grandmother", and that the pastry had been made from rank Irish butter; the malt was damnable, the sherry sour and the port, musty. I told the waiter to leave and sent Sir Philip to deal with the Lounger.'

'Which he did?'

'Oh, certainly,' said Harriet. 'I have never heard an old gentleman swear so fluently in my life before.'

'But I'll vow this Lounger left without paying.'

'Of course he did, in the manner of his kind, but not before Sir Philip had relieved him of his gold watch and chain.'

'I have fallen among thieves,' said the duke with a sudden smile.

The kitchen door opened and Sir Philip popped his head round, swore horribly when he saw who was in the kitchen, and disappeared.

'Is there anything I can do to help?' asked the duke.

'I think the best help you could give us at present would be to leave us alone,' said Harriet firmly.

'Meaning you, Miss James?'

'I and all of us. I am not at my best. This has been a terrible day. Rabbit masquerading as fowl will do only for an occasional dinner. The guests normally expect great joints of boiled beef, and so I must go to bed so that I can rise early and make preparations.'

She rose to her feet. He rose also and stood looking down at her, thinking how beautiful she appeared despite her fatigue.

'I would be your protector,' said the Duke of Rowcester.

Harriet's eyes flashed green fire. 'So your solution is to offer me a post as your mistress? Get you hence, your grace, before I really lose my temper. Do you not see, can you not see that for such as Mrs Budley and myself this hotel is saving us from indignities such as the one you have just dared to offer me?'

The door opened and Mrs Budley tripped in. She affected surprise at the sight of the duke, but it was done so amateurishly that both the duke and Harriet knew immediately that Sir Philip had told them up in the attics about the duke's presence in the kitchen.

'You should not be unchaperoned,' said Mrs Budley, colouring slightly at her own temerity, for the elegance and height of the duke awed her. 'Tea is ready for you in our little sitting room. I must ask you to come with me.'

'Gladly,' said Harriet. She swept a low curtsy to the duke, and picking the candle up from the kitchen table, she followed Mrs Budley out, leaving the duke in a darkness lit only by the glow from the dying fire.

He stood there for several minutes, wondering what clumsy devil had prompted him to offer her his protection. Then he turned on his heel and felt his way up the dark stone stairs to the hall above.

'Offered you carte blanche, hey?' demanded Sir Philip when he and the rest had heard Harriet's story. 'Why not take him up on it? Get a house on the Park, carriage, jewels.'

'How dare you suggest such a monstrous thing,' cried Lady Fortescue and rapped the old man hard

71

on the knuckles with the sticks of her fan. 'We must make attempts to keep him from the kitchen.'

Mrs Budley heaved a romantic sigh. 'But he is so very handsome. Where is he now?'

'Probably gone to Almack's,' said the colonel. 'You did the right thing, Miss James, and there is nothing like a good solid rebuff for driving a man off and keeping him away. He is no doubt paying court to some fair charmer at Almack's and has forgot your very existence.'

Harriet found this very depressing. To change the subject, she said to Sir Philip, 'You must stop advertising those teas in the coffee room, for it is simply too much work for me. Oh, I know I have help, but Mrs Bodge is a good plain cook, nothing more.'

'Can't get a chef cheap, not a good one,' said Lady Fortescue.

'Maybe, maybe,' said Sir Philip, thinking hard. 'I wish we could. Then we could keep Miss James away from the duke. I have a feeling he'll hang about here now just because of her.'

'Why should he?' demanded Lady Fortescue harshly. 'You have no idea how the ladies throw themselves at him. I have seen it on my visits to his home. Why waste time on Miss James when he can have any woman in London? Oh, Miss Tonks, do come off that horse!'

Miss Tonks was seated side-saddle on a large rocking-horse in the corner of what had once been the schoolroom, rocking to and fro in a dreamy way.

72

'Leave her,' said Sir Philip crossly. 'She's the only one of you that don't get on my nerves.'

Miss Tonks, deciding that the last person she wanted to champion her was Sir Philip, promptly got down from the horse.

'Do you think the Cadmans mean to pay?' she asked, sitting down next to Harriet. Sir Tristram Cadman and his family had booked only for a month, not for the whole Season. He had been drunk the day he arrived, and then had proceeded to drink great quantities of the hotel's champagne. His wife and daughter were always out shopping, and the day before, Mr Hamlit, the jeweller, had sent a man to demand payment for a pair of earrings. As the Cadmans had not been in London for very long, it was odd for such a famous jeweller to demand settlement so quickly, so it followed that Mr Hamlit had learned something unfavourable about the Cadmans.

'They *have* to pay,' cried Mrs Budley, her pansy-brown eyes at their widest. 'We would be ruined were we left with such a bill.'

'Perhaps, as we have only a small staff at night,' said the colonel, 'one of us should be keeping a watch on them. They may try to leave in the middle of the night.'

'I have taken certain precautions,' said Sir Philip with a grin. 'I searched their quarters when they were all down at dinner and found Sir Tristram had a bag of sovereigns, more than enough for their bill. So I wedged it down the back of the sofa in their sitting room.

'If they're honest, they'll scream for the missing money in the morning. You will search while l stand by with their bill. When you find the sovereigns, I present the bill. If they disappear during the night, we have the money anyway. How they pay their other creditors is their affair.'

'Now, that's clever,' said Miss Tonks. 'I could never think of anything like that.'

'Nor could you, featherhead,' said Sir Philip nastily.

Mrs Budley, to change the subject, looked across at the wooden horse, which was still moving back and forth gently on its rockers. 'Do you hear from your children these days, Lady Fortescue?' she asked.

'Hardly,' said Lady Fortescue bitterly. 'I gave birth to ten children, none of whom survived very long. That was my son Harry's horse. He died in my arms of scrofula when he was ten.'

Their voices rose and fell in Harriet's ears, but she hardly heard what they were saying. A waltz tune danced in her head. Was he at Almack's? Did he think of her?

The duke was at that moment dancing with London's latest beauty, Miss Valerie Simms. He had arrived at Almack's just before the doors closed at eleven. He had never liked Almack's, damning it as a shoddy place with bad refreshments, but this evening he found he was enjoying the glittering company, not one of whom would have dreamt of

74

working in a kitchen, even her own. Miss Simms had light brown hair, light brown eyes, a straight nose and a rosebud of a mouth. She floated in his arms and flirted to perfection. She would make a pretty and complacent wife. The duke did not like independent-minded women. Some men might affect to dislike the prattle of females but, he persuaded himself, he found it charming and stumbled only once when he was assailed with such a black cloud of boredom and such a longing to go back to the hotel that he forgot where he was. But the moment passed.

He must put Harriet James out of his mind. She was highly unsuitable. But . . . but what if her clothes caught fire at the kitchen hearth? Ridiculous to furnish a hotel and leave such an antique arrangement in the kitchen. He bowed to his partner, for the dance had finished, and then said, 'I wish to ask you something, Miss Simms.'

Her eyes glowed. Miss Simms knew herself to be belle of the ball. Now surely the Duke of Rowcester could only mean one thing . . . marriage.

'Your grace,' she murmured, 'you may ask me *anything.*'

'How long would it take to get a closed stove installed in a kitchen?'

Her face fell ludicrously. 'Your grace, I know nothing about stoves.'

'I should have known,' he said. 'I must find someone who does.'

He gracefully handed her over to her next partner

and then surveyed the company. Ladies caught his eye, fans flirted, eyes flirted, skirts were hitched just that little bit to show neat ankles. He needed a dowager, he thought, someone from the last century, when ladies were supposed to know more than their servants and do it better.

He saw old Lady Rumbelow and headed in her direction. 'Hey, what's this, Rowcester?' she hailed him. 'Come to ask me to dance, hey?'

'To ask your advice,' he said, sitting down next to her.

'He is asking about you,' squeaked Mrs Trust, Lady Rumbelow's daughter to *her* daughter, Fanny. 'We will walk towards them, not deliberately, mind, but as if we did not see them, and then you must make a pretty start of surprise. Open your eyes to their fullest and cry, "Why, Grandmama, I did not know you had company. What can this gentleman think of poor ickle *moi*?" Your grandmother will introduce you, and you must then sigh and say, "Ah, *quel dommage*, I have only this one dance left." Then he will ask you to dance.'

'A closed stove,' Lady Rumbelow was saying thoughtfully. 'The speed of installation depends on the money you are prepared to spend. Promise 'em the earth and they'll have it in in a trice. Send your man to Carter's in the Old Brompton Road. Ask him for a Winkle stove, they're the latest, ovens and all that, and a clockwork spit. Big thing, but very efficient.'

'It would need to be installed during the night-time,' said the duke, thinking that Harriet would not

76

appreciate a disruption of her kitchen during the day.

'Why not wait till the end of the Season?' demanded Lady Rumbelow. 'Heard the Bunbarys were in your house.'

'It's a present for a lady.'

'How romantic of you,' cackled Lady Rumbelow. 'Could I get this Carter person now?'

Lady Rumbelow said, 'It must be about one in the morning. But if you're that desperate, no doubt the man lives over his shop.'

'Thank you,' said the duke, and fled just before Mrs Trust and Fanny reached him.

Harriet rose as usual at six in the morning, washed and dressed and made her way down to the kitchen, quickening her step as she heard crashes and bangings echoing up from the basement.

She opened the door and stood amazed. A squad of workmen were hammering and banging. Where the open fire had been stood a large gleaming stove.

'Nearly finished, mum,' said the foreman. 'What about some beer?'

'But what are you doing?' cried Harriet. 'Who authorized this?'

'Duke of Rowcester, mum. Present for Lady Fortescue what owns this place.'

The duke had cleverly decided that after his proposition of the night before, Harriet James would not want to accept any present from him, even such a homely item as a kitchen range.

Harriet sat down suddenly at the table. Had he done this for her? He must have done. She would tell them to take it away. She did not want any favours from him. But, oh, what a difference it would make. And . . . and he had said it was a present for his aunt. So she rose and drew tankards of beer for the workmen.

Soon the fire was lit and the new stove was crackling merrily. Harriet looked at it dreamily, at the black gleaming surface, at the ovens at the side. Her small staff arrived and cried out in surprise at the transformation.

Then the workmen left and Harriet realized the work of the day had to begin.

All that long day she slaved away, looking up every time the kitchen door opened, thinking perhaps it might be the duke. She could hardly go and thank him, for the present had been for Lady Fortescue, and Lady Fortescue had told her she had already thanked her nephew but had warned Harriet, 'He is out to seduce you. The colonel and I have agreed that despite his generosity, we must do everything we can to dislodge him from the hotel.'

Sir Philip, ever practical, had decided the best way to help Harriet would be to find a chef. He was feeling very strong and wise, for had not the Cadmans slipped away during the night, and had he not retrieved that bag of sovereigns?

He took a carriage down to the Thames and stared out at the rotting hulks which housed the French prisoners. Among the hundreds imprisoned, there was probably at least a chef or two. He went into an unsavoury tavern by the river, feeling quite at home among the smelly, evil company, for he had been accustomed to frequenting such dives in his misspent youth.

He joined a group at a table and eased into the conversation, amazed once more at how well versed the members of the mob were with affairs of state. The talk was of the profligacy of the Prince of Wales and how his hopes to become Regent had been dashed by the recovery in health of his father, King George III, although, said one, looking round for informers, sedition being a crime, he reckoned the young prince could do no worse. After all, it was King George who had lost the American colonies through usury. The Prince of Wales wanted to fight France. Let him, he said. For his part, he thought it a good idea. It would boost morale, and if the prince was killed, the saving on the Privy Purse would be immense.

'Talking of the war,' said Sir Philip, 'do any of those Frenchies ever escape from the hulks?'

'One or two,' said a man who looked like a small muscular ape. 'But they don't get far, and they're catched for reward. No Englishman's going to let a Frog escape, and any man helping a Frog would be torn to pieces.'

Sir Philip gave a shudder despite the heat of the tavern. 'Forget about French prisoners,' he said hurriedly. 'I am looking for a French cook, and this is the wrong part of town.'

'Chefs, is it?' demanded the small man. 'Now Jake Mount, he catched a Frog and went for his reward, but the Frog says he's an emigrant and a chef to a man of quality; but they bangs him up just the same, him having barely the word o' English. Still, the military says he ain't one o' theirs and they get on to the fellow, Barlow, who the Frenchie says is his employer. "Aye," says Barlow, "I employed him but he stole two bottles of wine off of me", so Frenchie's banged up again. He comes up at the Bailey in an hour.'

Sir Philip called for a round of gin and hot water, paid his shot and made his escape. He went straight to the Old Bailey and wedged himself in among the press of people in the well of the court. He found himself jammed up against a large yokel at the bar who had been summoned for killing a woman of the town who had made an indecent assault on him in Chick Lane. He was severely cautioned to be more careful in future. Sir Philip shifted restlessly, jammed in as he was among prisoners, guards, witnesses and turnkeys. Up in the gallery was a packed throng of the beau monde come to see the sights: snapping snuff-boxes, fluttering fans, giggling, whispering and chattering like so many starlings on a roof. The stench was abominable, water was streaming down the walls and a thin mist from the river obscured the windows. On the judge's dais was a huge bunch of herbs to ward off gaol fever. Piemen were crying their wares at the door, and only the sullen prisoners were silent. The tedious day wore on. Forty-two felons were sentenced to be transported for seven years, four others to fourteen years and two persons to be branded as irrevocable vagabonds. And two poor women, after receiving a dreadful homily from the judge upon the enormity of subsisting without visible means of support, were ordered to be whipped for begging.

Then came the chef. His name was Paul Despard. He had only a few halting words of English. The judge was told he was charged with the theft of two bottles of wine from his employer, a Mr Barlow, but Mr Barlow was not in court. Despard was a skinny man with a white face and twisted mouth. 'Hang the Frog, demme,' cried one languid voice from the gallery, and the cry was taken up. One man after another reminded his neighbour that Frenchmen ate not only frogs but babies, Napoleon having one roasted for dinner every Sunday.

Sir Philip knew that if he did not move quickly, even if Despard got off, the crowd would tear the man to pieces.

Using his stick, he flogged right and left, clearing a space for himself until he was near enough to shout at the defence counsel, who was languidly picking his nose and staring gloomily at the crowd, 'I have something to say in this man's defence.'

Soon Sir Philip was in the witness-box, with his tortoise-like head poking over the top of it. In excellent French, he shouted to the prisoner, 'Leave it to me. Agree with everything I say.'

With a shudder he kissed the greasy Bible and took the oath.

'I am Sir Philip Sommerville,' he said. 'Paul Despard was to start employment with me at my hotel, The Poor Relation, an excellent establishment in Bond Street where the Duke of Rowcester is in residence, preferring the amenities of my excellent hotel to his own town house.'

'Get on with it, do,' sighed the judge.

'I am persuaded that Mr Barlow manufactured this trumped-up story about the theft of the wine because he was furious at this chef for leaving his employ. Besides, the so excellent Mr Barlow with his contempt for British justice is not even here. (And I hope he isn't, prayed Sir Philip.) Paul Despard escaped the terrors of the French Revolution ten years ago. He was a loyal subject of the French king. He is now a loyal subject of King George. Let every man jack in this court show this poor foreigner that we in England are just and fair, that we have no tribunals here. Cry God for justice, freedom, England and King George!' cried Sir Philip, jumping up and down with almost Shakespearian fervour.

A great cheer rent the court and went on, almost drowning out the verdict of 'not guilty', given by a jury who had not bothered to retire to consider their decision.

Fortunately for Sir Philip, who then wondered if he would be able to get near Despard to take him away, the poor women prisoners provided a more interesting diversion, as quality and hoi polloi alike poured out of the court to see them stripped and flogged at Bridewell.

Sir Philip, finally having secured the person of Despard, led him out of the Old Bailey and so down to Ludgate Hill, which was thronged with carriages and chairs, and with mercers' shops bright with silks and muslins.

'In here,' said Sir Philip, stopping outside a tavern in Fleet Street. He ordered ale and a meat pie for Despard, and then sat back and studied the Frenchman. Whether he had suffered an apoplexy at some time or had been born that way, his mouth was twisted down at the left-hand side, giving his dead-white face a perpetual sneer. He was dirty and lice-ridden after his sojourn in Newgate. Sir Philip sighed. He would need to get the fellow washed before he presented him to Harriet.

So far, Despard had remained silent, but after he had wolfed down the meat pie, cramming the pastry into his mouth with dirty fingers, he said very carefully in English, 'Thank you.'

Sir Philip's beady eyes saw the faint scars on the man's wrists and he said, in French, 'When did you escape?'

The Frenchman gave a hiss of dismay and rose to his feet, but Sir Philip pulled him down again. 'Do you think I'm going to hand you back after having got you out? I'm interested, that's all. You have nothing to fear by telling me. Who is this Barlow?'

Bit by bit, Despard's story came out. He had indeed been a prisoner on one of the hulks. Some humanitarians had come on board one day to inspect the prisoners, and several of the healthier ones had been taken up on deck for inspection. Their chains had been removed for the visit. Despard, at the end of the line, had seen his chance and had slipped overboard, climbing down the side of the hulk and so into the waters of the Thames. He had swum ashore. There had been gossip among the prisoners of a certain Mr Evans who ran a servant agency and who was sympathetic to the French. It was said he would help any who managed to escape to find employ. Despard had hidden in his shoe one gold louis which he sold in a backstreet and obtained enough for food, drink, paper and pen. He had written out the name of Mr Evans and had proceeded to ask for directions, pointing to his mouth to show that he was dumb, for he was afraid his few words of broken English and strong French accent would give him away.

And so he had ended up at the agency in Amen Lane in the City. Evans had been kind and helpful. He had supplied the Frenchman with clean clothes and a hot meal and had then sent him to a merchant's house to take up the post as chef. The merchant was a Mr Barlow. Despard said Barlow must have known he was an escaped prisoner, for not only had he made him work as chef but as scullery maid and pot-boy as well. There were no wages. Despard had guessed that the generous Mr Evans was in fact a crook who found servants for employers for a fat fee, the employers paying him in lieu of paying any wages. Despard had protested. Barlow said if he left, he would tell the authorities he was an escaped prisoner. Despard was intelligent enough to point out that that would make Barlow a collaborator. It was then that Barlow had smiled and said he would report him as a common thief. Despard had fled. Some of the mob were passing him in the street and one tripped him up. He had cried out in French and they had seized him and taken him to the nearest round-house. He was not surprised that the military authorities had not known of his disappearance, for the lazy captain of the hulk did not keep an accurate tally of the many prisoners who died, and Despard had had no papers on him when he was arrested. In desperation he gave Barlow's name, hoping Barlow would protect himself by protecting him, but Barlow had given the trumped-up charge of theft of two bottles of wine.

'Can you cook?' asked Sir Philip.

'I am the son of a Paris restaurateur,' he said. 'I know my trade. I was a chef in my father's restaurant before I was pressed into the army.'

'Well, let's hope you're good enough after all this,' said Sir Philip with feeling. 'I'm tired.' He wondered, not for the first time, at the stamina of Lady Fortescue and Colonel Sandhurst.

Harriet felt like a complete amateur as she watched Paul Despard take over the running of the kitchen. He worked at amazing speed. He seemed able to cook several dishes at once and still have time to sit down and drink a leisurely glass of wine. She would have liked to stay on and watch this genius at work and help him, but Sir Philip said he had not spent a poxy day at the Bailey just to see her carrying on in drudgery, and so for the first time since the hotel opened, Harriet found herself with leisure time, in fact, more than any of the others, as – by general consensus – she was expected to stay upstairs, out of sight of the duke. So she helped Betty and John, Lady Fortescue's servants, with the chores of looking after the other five partners of The Poor Relation, and often stood by the attic windows of the school-room in the evenings to watch society going out to play.

The place the Cadmans had left in the hotel was taken by Lord and Lady Darkwood and their daughters. Harriet was on one of her rare visits to the kitchens when she met Lady Darkwood on the stairs, and both stared at each other in surprise. For Lady Darkwood was none other than the former Miss Susan Danesmith, whom Harriet had known briefly in her debutante days. She was about to pass her when Susan held out both hands, crying, 'It *is* you. I said to Darkwood, "Would it not be fun if the Harriet James who is a partner here is my Harriet!"'

'When I heard Lord and Lady Darkwood were here with their two daughters,' said Harriet, 'I did not know you had married, and I thought the daughters must be debutantes.'

'Hardly. Margaret is four and Belinda, two. Come, come into my sitting room and take tea. You must tell me all, and how you come to be here.'

Susan was a tall, statuesque blonde with fair skin

only slightly pitted by smallpox, and large, square, brownish teeth.

'I am still as clumsy as ever, Harriet,' she said. 'The handles just fall off vases when I touch them.' She laughed merrily and Harriet felt a spasm of guilt, knowing that the breakages were due to Sir Philip's machinations rather than Susan's clumsiness. Lady Darkwood rang the bell for tea and Miss Tonks answered its summons, the poor relations continuing the wait on the bedchambers to provide their upper-class guests with the charm of being served by their own kind. Harriet introduced her. Once tea was served, she told Susan of her adventures, or rather, her lack of adventures until she had met Lady Fortescue.

'What a famous lark!' laughed Susan. 'But what do you do for social life?'

'Being in trade removes me from society.'

'I suppose it does,' said Susan heartlessly. 'Oh, I do envy you, pretending to be a chef and everything.'

'I was a chef through necessity, dear Susan. I am not like Marie Antoinette. I am one of the world's workers.'

'How adventurous. I do admire you so much. It would be amusing just to see what it's like to be poor if only for the littlest time, because I might become unfashionable like you and then no one would invite me anywhere. Of course, you could come to Lady Stanton's ball with me, if you like,' said Susan, rattling on, seeming to find Harriet's tales of poverty highly amusing. 'Darkwood won't go. So tiresome. He's overseeing the alterations to our town house.'

'Even if I wanted to go,' said Harriet, 'it would not do your social consequence any good to be seen with a hotelier, and one whom you had taken into society.'

'It's a masked ball. Keep your mask on. No one will know. We shall giggle and flirt like the old days. Everyone I know is so boring and wouldn't be seen *dead* working in a hotel.'

'And nor should they,' said Harriet with a reluctant smile. 'That is why they are *in* society and I am *out.*'

'Oh, do come with me. I told Lady Stanton that Darkwood would not come and I would probably be forced to bring some female with me. So all is right and tight. La Stanton is in alt because Rowcester has accepted her invitation. Do you remember that ball when he could not take his eyes off you? What a laugh! Of course, he can't look at you now, you having fallen from grace, although, my darling Harriet, in the *decentest* way possible. Does he know you are here? Has he seen you?'

'Yes, we exchanged a few words,' said Harriet bleakly. 'His aunt is one of the partners, too.'

'Yes, of course, but she is accounted in her dotage. She quite terrifies me as she and that colonel *creak* about the dining room like a pair of animated mummies.'

Why am I sitting here, listening to Susan's artless, heartless prattle? wondered Harriet. But she could not help thinking of that ball. Just once more, just one more time of being perfumed and gowned. Just one more waltz.

'Do you *have* a ballgown?' she realized Susan was saying.

'Yes. Only one left. It is the one I wore at that last ball before my poor parents died.'

'If you haven't worn it since, why, no one will recognize it,' said Susan. 'I remember it. It was white.'

'Suitable for a young miss,' said Harriet. 'Perhaps I shall trim it with some colour.'

'Good. That's settled. Come and meet my darling children. I quite dote on them. But I shall not have any more, and so I told Darkwood. London is full of harlots, and so I told him, why trouble me? Men are so odd, are they not? He became quite incensed and called me unfeeling. Can you imagine? I am all sensibility. I faint if I see a cat in distress.'

But not a hanging, thought Harriet cynically. Sensibility was all the rage. A certain Lady Harman had gone into deep mourning for the death of her lap-dog, following a special funeral cortège up the Edgware Road where bodies hung from the gibbets in chains like rotting fruit. But to cry for anyone on the scaffold would be regarded as vulgarity.

Harriet's calm announcement that she was to attend Lady Stanton's ball was met with suspicion. Was Rowcester to be there?

'I think not,' lied Harriet. 'It is a masked ball, so no one will know me.'

'Good,' said Lady Fortescue, 'for if you were recognized, then you would be in disgrace for having had the temerity to show your face, and that would not do our business here any good at all. People should know their place,' she added without a gleam of humour. 'I am glad Rowcester is not to be there, for although the present of the range was magnificent, it made me uneasy. I fear he means to make you his mistress after all, Miss James, and as Sir Philip has gone out of his way to produce a French cook, the least you can do to reward him is to keep out of the duke's way and remain a respectable lady.'

'I have no intention of becoming the Duke of Rowcester's mistress,' said Harriet evenly.

'Indeed, Lady Fortescue,' protested little Mrs Budley timidly, 'you should know our dear Miss James would never stoop so low.'

'A duke is a duke,' said Lady Fortescue awfully. 'We really must try to dislodge him from this hotel.'

'It's a wonder he hasn't tried to buy us out,' said Sir Philip. 'Did he not say anything on the matter, Lady Fortescue?'

He apologized for having thought me mad,' said Lady Fortescue, playing with the fringes of her fan. 'He offered to set me up at a place in the country, but I refused. We must all stick together.'

There was more to it than that, thought Sir Philip, eyeing her narrowly. I wouldn't be surprised if he'd offered to buy us out and she refused because this all amuses her and she don't want to go off to the country and die.

Instead he said, 'Who's keeping the account books?'

'I am,' said Colonel Sandhurst.

'May as well turn them back over to Miss James,' said Sir Philip. 'You ain't the best with figures, Colonel.'

'I am sure Miss James will find all in order.'

But Harriet, poring over the books late that night, was appalled by the great amount of expense from the kitchen in such a short time. Genius he might be, but Paul Despard must be taught economy. She went down to the kitchen to talk to him. In the hall, the Duke of Rowcester was standing chatting to a lady whose pretty daughters gazed adoringly up at him. The duke saw Harriet and gave her a stiff nod before turning back to what he obviously considered pleasant company. Harriet looked at the fine gowns of the ladies and was miserably conscious of her own black dress and muslin apron and starched cap.

Lady Fortescue might rest easy, Harriet thought in a dejected way. The duke had no intention of pursuing her, which, as Harriet firmly told her depressed spirits, was a Very Good Thing.

FIVE

Thou know'st the mask of night is on my face,
Else would a maiden blush bepaint my cheek.

WILLIAM SHAKESPEARE

The duke's offer to make her his mistress should have given Harriet a disgust of him – as it had, she fiercely told herself. The heavy, languorous feeling she had when she thought about him she put down to dismay that she should socially have sunk so low. She worked away in the evenings on her old ball gown, trimming it with bows of green silk and making herself a green silk mask, but thinking as she stitched that it was folly to go to the ball. She had been so grateful to Lady Fortescue for having ended her dreary days of isolation. But this ball might bring back all the old misery and discontent.

When Lady Darkwood sent for her on the day before the ball, she appeared flurried and upset. 'Darkwood is being an old pig,' she burst out. 'I told him I was taking you to the ball and he said it was the outside of enough and I was shaming the Darkwood name, just as if his father hadn't been an ironmaster and bought his title!'

Now was the opportunity for Harriet to say it was all right, that she did not really want to go anyway, to deny that each stitch set among the green silk bows had carried a memory of that waltz with the duke, but instead she said lightly, 'Then you must tell Darkwood I am not going, Susan. He will be none the wiser when I *do* go.'

Susan clapped her hands. 'Wicked puss! We shall both go and be wicked together, for my husband will not be here when we do leave. Everyone is desperate to see if Rowcester pays court to Lady Stanton.'

'Why?' asked Harriet.

'She has been telling all that will listen she means to make him her own and she has the edge on the young misses, for she plans to get him to bed if she cannot get him to the altar.'

'How very forward,' said Harriet primly. 'I am sure the Duke of Rowcester who, 'tis said, hardly ever attends the Season, is come this time to find a wife. He will not be interested in elderly widows.'

Susan cackled with laughter. 'You obviously have not seen her. She is our age and quite stupendously beautiful, not like the dewy Miss Simms, mark you, but in a full-blown, bold way. And she breaks hearts.'

Once again a voice in Harriet's head urged her not to go, but she said nothing. That evening, Miss Tonks and Mrs Budley wistfully admired the finished gown. 'Have a dance for each of us,' said Mrs Budley. 'We shall never have the chance to go into society again.'

'You shall if this hotel is a success,' said Sir Philip.

'Enough money for us all to retire and then relaunch ourselves.'

Miss Tonks brightened and then her face fell. 'There are six of us. Once the money is divided up, none of us will be rich enough for society to forgive us.'

'Hark at you,' sneered Sir Philip. 'Remembering those days when you were belle of the ball?'

Miss Tonks remembered vividly days when she had been a wallflower, and burst into tears.

'I have a good mind to call you out,' snarled the colonel.

'Why don't you look in your own glass,' said Lady Fortescue, 'and see what an ugly little satyr you are become.'

To everyone's amazement, Sir Philip burst into tears as well. He had never cared for anyone's opinion of him before, but Lady Fortescue's remarks had cut him to the bone.

Mrs Budley, who was gently sentimental, began to cry quietly as well.

'I thought we were all friends,' exclaimed Harriet. 'Friends do not insult and wound each other.'

'There, now,' said Sir Philip, after blowing his nose, 'I should not tease you, Miss Tonks, and I am heartily sorry.'

'And I only said that to wound you, Sir Philip,' said Lady Fortescue. 'As a matter of fact, you have become quite the peacock these days.'

Sir Philip dried his eyes on a grubby handkerchief, preened and adjusted his enormous cravat.

'Now that is going too far,' murmured the colonel, sotto voce, to Lady Fortescue.

'Oh, he's quite a game little cock,' whispered Lady Fortescue. 'He had the temerity to kiss me.'

'The deuce!' exclaimed the colonel angrily and glared at Sir Philip fiercely.

The duke, returning from his club, had been unfortunate enough to have heard the gossip about Lady Stanton's ambitions. He wondered whether he should cancel his acceptance. As he approached the hotel on foot, he could see the carriages outside and hear the hum of conversation from inside.

He knew his very presence was attracting customers. He should leave. He had visited the kitchen, hoping he might be welcomed by a grateful Harriet, but had found instead a sinister-looking French chef. He had seen Harriet only briefly, once as she was crossing the hall to go down to the kitchens, and once as she was darting lightly up the stairs.

Although he persuaded himself that the reason he was staying on was to talk Lady Fortescue into accepting his generous offer, he felt in his heart of hearts that she would never accept. He had offered to buy all of them out, but Lady Fortescue had thanked him warmly and said she was now interested in the hotel and would rather wait to see what happened, begging him not to mention his offer to any of the others.

Stubborn old harridan, he thought. And the rest of them were disgraceful in the way they were trying to dislodge him; nothing overt, just a sort of dumb insolence all round, even from that faded spinster, Tonks, who kept telling him ad nauseam that he would be more comfortable in his own home.

And yet, despite Sir Philip's tricks with the china and furniture, the hotel was very well run, and a haven for *ton* families who would have shunned the other, more masculine hotels. That French chef, whoever he might be, was superb, and his dinners were beginning to be the talk of London. The Prince of Wales's friends had dined there the other night, and rumour had it that Prinny himself might drop in.

After dinner, the duke went back to his club and spent a leisurely hour or two gambling, withdrawing only when he considered the stakes were becoming ridiculously high. He had no wish to see all his hard work on the estates vanishing over the gaming tables of White's.

He strolled back to Bond Street, his sword-stick always at the ready, for despite diligent patrolling by the militia, there was no telling when the mob might erupt into the West End. There was the mob who favoured the war in the Peninsula and would break the windows of any house not showing candles after a victory. Then there was the anti-war mob who might do the same thing to any house visibly celebrating a victory and who were apt to take their rage out on any well-dressed man walking the streets. The duke showed his cuffs, a brave thing to do in an age when most men had their sleeves cut long to hide their linen, for somehow it was that band of white, that band which separated gentleman from commoner, that drove the mob to more fury than any show of jewels.

The hotel was hushed and quiet, with only one porter sleeping on a chair by the door. Society was still out at its pleasures.

He saw Harriet at the back of the hall. She gave him a veiled look and then slipped through the door that led down to the kitchen.

He restrained an urge to follow her. He had bought the stove which, after all, had not benefited her but some villainous Frenchman. To the devil with her, he thought, suddenly angry. He went up to his room.

Down in the kitchen, Harriet swung a large pot of water onto the new stove and stirred up the fire. When she had announced to Mrs Budley and Miss Tonks her intention of going down to the kitchen to wash all over, they had exclaimed in dismay, and with more dismay when they learned she meant to wash her hair as well. Rice powder brushed through the hair, they said, was sufficient to clean it, and washing all over was necessary only when one had had the fever. Miss Tonks said proudly that she had taken a bath in March and would think about one again the next September, for she was 'notoriously clean'.

But Miss Tonks, thought Harriet, was not going to a ball, nor had she been sweating in the kitchen for weeks before the chef arrived.

The members of society simply poured on more

scent the ranker they became, and although Lady Fortescue and the colonel managed to keep fairly sweet-smelling, Harriet found her nostrils were becoming increasingly offended not only by the smells of others but by the smell of herself.

She unhitched a tin hip bath from the back door and placed it in front of the fire and, when the water was boiling, tipped it in and then filled it up with cold water until she had reached the desired temperature.

She had no fear of being disturbed, for the partners and servants had strict instructions not to go near the kitchen for an hour and the chef had gone to his lodgings.

Harriet sprinkled rose water into the bath, and then stripped off all her clothes and laid them over a chair before lowering herself into the water. Miss Tonks had presented her with a bar of Joppa soap. Harriet soaped herself all over and then poured water over her hair from the several jugs she had placed beside the bath to rinse herself, and washed her long black tresses thoroughly.

Then she stood up and leaned down and picked up another jug of water and let the contents cascade over her hair and down her body – just as the duke opened the door and walked in.

He stood stock-still. She had her naked back to him. Her beautiful body was lit with a pinkish glow from the red embers in the fire shining out of the open stove door. Rivulets of soap ran down her body.

He was seized with such a wave of longing, such a desire to cross the floor and hold that naked, wet body against his own that his hands began to tremble. And yet, in the same instant, he knew that if she turned round and saw him, she would never forgive him.

Somehow he managed to leave softly and quietly, closing the door so gently behind him that she was never aware that anyone had been there.

He gained the hall and stood for a moment, blinking in the light of the chandelier, which seemed to be the focus of an infuriated lady's attention. 'That's *our* chandelier,' she hissed. 'That old wretch tricked you out of it. Where is Sir Philip?'

The duke walked up the stairs, wondering which of Sir Philip's infuriated relatives the lady and gentleman would prove to be. That image of naked Harriet seemed to be burned into his brain, so much so that he nearly collided with Susan, Lady Darkwood.

'La, your grace!' exclaimed Susan. 'It must be love, you are so abstracted.'

'Not I,' said the duke gallantly. 'I was merely stunned by your beauty.'

'Naughty man! But you must promise to dance with me at Lady Stanton's ball tomorrow night.'

'Alas, I cannot. I have quite decided to cancel my invitation.'

'Everything is going wrong,' she said pettishly. 'I have a mind not to go myself, for Darkwood raised such a dust when I said I was taking Miss James. "Going out in society with a cook," he sneered. But Miss James cleverly pointed out that I should say she

99

was not going, and that way *he* would be comfortable and we could have such a good time. I quite dote on Miss James, although she has become a trifle severe and sad in manner and not like her old self, but that is probably caused by slaving over the pots and pans. So vulgar! Perhaps Darkwood has the right of it. But it is to be masked, you know, and no one would recognize her, and if one did not recognize her, one would never take her for a cook. Still . . .'

'I was teasing you,' said the duke, interrupting this flow. 'I shall be there. You may have your dance.'

'But how will you know me? I shall be masked like everyone else.'

'Dear Lady Darkwood – your figure, your grace, your charm, your style, how could I make a mistake?'

'Wicked, wicked man,' laughed Susan, highly delighted, not knowing that he was cruelly adding in his mind, 'and your brown teeth, and your silly laugh.'

'But you must not tell Miss James that I am to be there,' he said, 'for it might upset her to know that a guest from this hotel was to be present and might recognize her.'

'I shall not breathe a word,' said Susan. 'In fact, I shall tell her you are *not* going.'

'Splendid,' he said, bowed, and moved on past her up to his room.

But Susan, as she went downstairs, thought it odd that he should be so anxious to reassure Harriet that he would not be there because he was a guest at the hotel, considering that most of the other hotel guests would be there. Still, it would be wonderful to make Lady Stanton jealous when she had that dance. So she would tell Harriet he was not going.

She did not, however, remember to tell Harriet this news until Harriet had joined her in her rooms, preparatory to leaving for the ball.

Harriet's cheeks were flushed with excitement. She had paraded in her ballgown for the others, and all, even Sir Philip – although he was still smarting under the insults cast at him by Mrs Tommy Brickhampton, who had only been persuaded to depart after a promise to pay for the wretched chandelier – had said she looked beautiful. The gown of white muslin over a pale green underdress of silk was embellished with a green silk sash and little green silk bows like butterflies on her shoulders. Miss Tonks, who was clever at such things, had fashioned a coronet of green silk roses from a piece of material she had 'put by', and Harriet did not know the sad tears Miss Tonks had shed as the shears had plunged into that lovely silk which she had been treasuring for her own ballgown. With the first cut, she had known she was cutting all her hopes of romance finally out of her life.

'Oh, you are prettier than I,' complained Susan, 'and that is not at all the thing, seeing as how I am risking my social reputation by taking you. I wish I had worn green instead of blue. I did not realize touches of green could be so very fetching. It's just not fair!'

Harriet's assurances that Susan's blue gown and sapphire tiara would make Lady Stanton die of jealousy restored Susan's mercurial spirits. 'I had quite forgot. Rowcester will not be there, so he must have heard all the rumours about La Stanton's intentions of setting her cap at him.'

Well, he was not going after all, thought Harriet. And she had really always thought he would not go. The depression that assailed her was because of the strain of the past weeks.

'That is a lovely scent you are wearing,' said Susan. 'What is it?'

'Soap. I had a bath last night.'

'Are you ill?'

'I had a desire to be clean.'

'My maid rubs me down with a flannel,' said Susan. 'Quite sufficient, I assure you. Now come along. Martha' – to her maid – 'our cloaks, please, and carry our fans and reticules out to the carriage.'

I once took all this for granted, thought Harriet as a footman helped her into the Darkwoods' well-sprung carriage. She tried to forget her present life and imagine that she was once more the adored daughter of doting parents. But the thought of her dead parents made her feel sad, so, with a little sigh, she turned her attention to Susan's gossip.

'You see, I have been thinking a lot about you,' said Susan. 'When the Season is over, if I cannot beg Darkwood to take me to Brighton, back we go to the country, back to dreary Sussex and that great barn of a place to yawn my head off day in and day out, and everyone for miles around seems to be in their dotage. Something to do with the climate. It keeps people alive for much too long. Consider Lady Fortescue, for instance. She should have been decently tucked up in her coffin this age, although I do not believe she hails from Sussex originally. I think the Fortescues were Kent. So what I was thinking is this. Why not come with me as companion and leave this sordid hotel trade? What larks we would have! I tell you, they are not all tottering on the edge of the grave in Sussex. In fact, there is a delicious young man who visits from time to time, a Mr Courtney. Such legs, my dear. Like balustrades, I assure you. Every time I see those legs, my heart goes pit-a-pat.'

'Did not your heart go pit-a-pat for Darkwood?' asked Harriet.

'Stoopid. One does not *love* one's husband. One takes lovers *after* marriage, which is the benefit of marriage and about the only one I can think of, because all husbands do, when they are not in the House or at their club or on the hunting field, is expect one to breed. So tiresome, don't you think? Yes, you shall come with me, Harriet, and we shall set Sussex by the heels.'

'It is very kind of you, very kind indeed,' said Harriet awkwardly. 'But, indeed, I am tied to Lady Fortescue.'

'Never say you are a bonded servant!' squeaked Susan.

'I was thinking of the ties of loyalty and gratitude.'

'Oh, *those*. Put them quite out of your head.'

'May I consider your proposal?' asked Harriet, more to stem the flow than from any determination even to consider being a companion to this rattle-pate.

'By all means. But I have no doubt you will come about. The hotel is great fun as a novelty, but you would not like it to go on for *years*, now would you? Look, we are arrived. Is my mask straight?'

'Yes, Susan.'

'And what do I look like?'

'Wickedly alluring.'

Susan giggled appreciatively.

I *should* be her companion, thought Harriet. I lie so well.

They descended from the carriage and through a double row of footmen into the entrance hall. 'Did you mark those footmen?' whispered Susan. 'All matched in height.'

Harriet's spirits, which had been low, lifted to the sound of the music filtering down from the ballroom upstairs. They went into a dressing room off the hall and Susan's correct maid helped them out of their mantles.

'I forgot,' hissed Susan urgently, 'you cannot be announced as Miss James. Here, what shall we call you?' She fumbled in her reticule and took out her card case and a silver pencil. 'See, I shall write Miss Something-or-other under my own name. I have it! Miss Venus, how is that?'

'Sounds like an actress or an opera dancer,' said

Harriet reprovingly. 'I know; Mama's maiden name was Ward. Miss Ward will do.'

'How dull, but Miss Ward it is. Now you must not dance off and abandon me or I shall be cross!'

But no sooner were they in the ballroom than Susan eagerly hailed her friends, the ones that were carrying face masks on little poles and could therefore be easily recognized, and left Harriet on her own.

Harriet looked about nervously. She, too, recognized many people but could not hail them because of the social disgrace that would result from her even being there.

She recognized the Duke of Rowcester despite his black velvet mask. He was dancing with Lady Stanton, who was almost as tall as he. She was holding a mask on a jewelled stick in front of her face but dropping it from time to time so that the duke could receive the full effect of her beauty. And she *was* beautiful, thought Harriet. Fair hair was damned as unfashionable, but the duke did not seem to have noticed that. Lady Stanton's blonde locks were dressed in a Roman style under a headdress of ostrich plumes. Her gown was of gold tissue, damped to her body. She had heavy-lidded eyes and a lazy, caressing gaze.

Harriet looked about for Susan, but Susan was already dancing with a guardsman and seemed to have forgotten Harriet's very existence.

Harriet suddenly wished she had not come. It was agony to be on the outside looking in, no longer a real part of this glittering scene. She decided to go and sit quietly in the corner beside some dowager and wait patiently, unobserved, until the evening was over.

A very old lady was half asleep behind a stand of hothouse flowers. There was an empty chair next to her. Harriet went and sat down. The old lady roused herself. 'Evening,' she said harshly. 'Name's Rumbelow.'

'I am Miss Ward,' said Harriet.

'Well, Miss Ward, and what are you doing sitting next to an old crone like me? Are all the young men blind?'

'I came as Lady Darkwood's companion,' said Harriet, 'but I do not feel like dancing.'

'Just as well, perhaps,' said Lady Rumbelow. 'Loose affairs, these masked balls. The very presence of masks gets everyone excited, as if no one could tell who they are. Lady Stanton don't even bother to cover her face, she's so busy flirting with Rowcester. Wasting her time there.'

'Why do you say that? Lady Stanton is extremely beautiful.'

'He won't notice. He's very unromantic.'

'Indeed. Perhaps that is why he is not married. But why do you say he is unromantic?'

Lady Rumbelow cackled and then said, 'He was at the first subscription ball at Almack's. All the beauties were there. Not Lady Stanton, mind you, because the patronesses don't let her have vouchers, for she quarrelled with one of them, can't remember

106

which. Where was I? Ah, yes, well, Rowcester was dancing with the latest belle, Miss Simms, and I heard later, he asked if he might ask her something. She of course thought he meant to pop the question in the middle of Almack's, but he ups and asks her where he can get a stove. *She* don't know. Her generation can't even blow their noses. So he comes to me and I send him to Carter's. Mark this!' Lady Rumbelow nudged Harriet in the ribs with one pointed elbow. 'He wants to present this stove to a lady, and so determined is he that he rushes out of Almack's to go and rouse the stove man.'

A warm glow started somewhere in the pit of Harriet's stomach. He had thought of her, he had thought enough of her to go out in the middle of the night to find that stove. But he was smiling down into Lady Stanton's eyes, his eyes glinting behind his mask, and how beautifully they danced together! He probably thinks of me as a charity case, reflected Harriet, the warm glow dying away.

'Oh, Lor', here's m' granddaughter,' said Lady Rumbelow as Miss Fanny Trust came tripping up. 'Enjoying yourself?' she said to Fanny.

'Tolerable well,' replied Fanny. 'All the talk is of Rowcester. Is he here?'

'Of course he's here, you widgeon, dancing with Lady Stanton. No other man here has legs like that.'

'You must introduce me,' said Fanny firmly.

'May I present Miss Ward? Miss Ward, Miss Trust,' said Lady Rumbelow, deliberately misunderstanding her.

'I mean Rowcester,' pouted Fanny. 'You had him at Almack's and let him get away.'

'I could hardly chain him to the floor, could I?' remarked her grandmother. 'The dance is over. Drift elegantly in his direction. No, wait. He has asked Lady Darkwood for a dance and she is giggling in that awful way she has. Beg pardon, Miss Ward, I had forgot she was your friend. Ah, here's a beau for you, Fanny. Young Daventry, if I am not mistook.'

A young man in a scarlet mask bowed before Fanny, caught sight of Harriet, and stood irresolute. Lady Rumbelow took pity on him. 'You were about to ask my granddaughter to dance, were you not, Mr Daventry?'

'Yes, yes.' He wrenched his eyes away from Harriet with an effort. 'If I might be so bold as to crave an introduction to . . .'

'After your dance,' said Lady Rumbelow. 'Off with you.'

'Smitten the moment he saw you,' she said to Harriet after the pair had walked off. 'But I have to look after my own flesh and blood.'

Harriet's eyes followed not Fanny and Mr Daventry, but the Duke of Rowcester. She was confident that she could barely be seen behind the barrier of hothouse plants. Mr Daventry must have followed Fanny, for he could not have seen her from the ballroom once she had begun to talk to her grandmother.

The duke and Susan were now dancing the cotillion, Susan making the most of every chance to flirt when the figure of the dance brought them together.

And then, as Harriet watched, the duke said something, Susan laughed and looked about, then shrugged in an I-don't-know sort of way. The duke continued to dance with elegance and grace, but his eyes raked round the ballroom and Harriet wondered breathlessly if he was looking for her.

'What do you think of Fanny?' she realized Lady Rumbelow was asking her.

'Miss Trust? She is a very pretty lady.'

'But my daughter has quite ruined her. She showed all signs of having a brain behind that pretty face when she was a child, but that was looked on with alarm. She was taught to lisp, speak bad French and baby-talk. What will happen to her after marriage? What will happen to a young woman with only an empty, uneducated brain for company?'

'You are very modern in your views,' said Harriet. 'It is well known that gentlemen do not like intelligent women. She will have many children to keep her occupied.'

The old lady stared at her in surprise. 'But after the birth the wet-nurse and then the nursery maid take over, followed by a governess or tutor. What gently bred young lady ever spends time with her children? Why, here's Rowcester. Get your stove?'

The duke bowed. 'Thank you, Lady Rumbelow.'

'Well, Rowcester, this here is Miss Ward. You may take her for a dance, if that is your intention.'

For a moment the duke was dismayed, thinking he

had not found Harriet, but the eyes looking up at him were as green as a cat's and that glossy black hair could not belong to anyone else.

'Miss Ward,' he said, his eyes dancing, 'may I have the honour?'

Harriet rose and took his arm. As he led her to the floor, she was aware of watching eyes, of Susan, of Lady Stanton, and of the sudden buzz of speculation.

'A waltz, Miss Ward,' he said. 'Not yet sanctioned by Almack's, but I feel somehow we have danced it before.'

As he put his arm at her waist, he was vividly reminded of what she had looked like naked, and only her little gasp of surprise recalled him to his senses and made him realize he was pulling her against his body instead of holding her the regulation twelve inches away. Harriet let the music flow over her and around her. She forgot about the hotel, about the other poor relations, and lived only for each moment of that dance. If anyone had told her that her rapture was because of the duke's hand at her waist, she would have been horrified. She would have said she was losing herself in a secure past when her mother and father were alive and she was making her debut. But when she curtsied to him at the end of the dance, the present rushed back on her, the avid, curious eyes glinting through masks, the fluttering fans and the fact that she was now in trade and should therefore not be at the ball at all.

'Supper, I think,' said the duke easily, leading her towards the refreshment room. Well, as Susan was to

110

point out later, she need not have gone. He could hardly have dragged her there in front of everyone.

The refreshments were a copy of those served at Vauxhall Gardens: wafers of Westphalia ham and rack punch. Harriet was very hungry, for with all the preparation for the ball, she had not had time to eat, but her appetite appeared to have gone, so she drank rack punch on an empty stomach. The powerful drink had the effect of relaxing her and so, when he said, 'I know it is you, Miss James,' she was able to reply calmly, 'Masks are not a very good disguise, but I hope no one else recognizes me or Lady Darkwood would never be forgiven.'

'It is ridiculous, your having to hide like this,' he said, 'although you have brought it on yourself.'

'Your grace, in my all-too-recent state of genteel poverty I had as little hope then of being accepted in society as I do now. I am practically an ape leader and have no dowry.'

'Perhaps there is some man to whom your lack of dowry would not matter.'

'In society?' She laughed. 'Even if there were such a one besotted enough, his parents, relatives or lawyers would soon step in to stop it.'

'A man in love would not bow down before any pressure.'

'Fiddlesticks. You yourself were out to ruin the hotel because of the disgrace of having a relative as a hotelier. I have it on good authority that love has nothing to do with marriage.'

'Which authority?'

'Lady Darkwood, for one.'

'That rattle? Not suitable company. She has few morals.'

'Lady Darkwood is extremely kind and is risking her reputation by bringing me here.'

He leaned back in his chair and studied her. She did not blush or turn her head away from him but regarded him steadily and curiously through the slits in her mask.

'Did Lady Fortescue tell you that I had offered to buy all of you out?'

Harriet looked surprised. 'I understood the offer was to take care of *her*. No, she did not mention it. But, as I warned you, the hotel has given her new life, as has it done to us all. We squabble occasionally, but we are like a family and very loyal to each other.'

'Folly. Pure folly. What if I should offer you the sum I was prepared to pay to buy you all out? That would furnish you with an excellent dowry. Think on it, Miss James – once more restored to your place.'

Harriet looked about her, and several hard, curious eyes stared back. She gave a little sigh. 'Perhaps my soul belongs to the merchant class now. Seen from outside, society seems . . . shoddy. Lady Rumbelow was concerned about her granddaughter's future. She is worried that after marriage, Miss Trust will have nothing to occupy her time or make up for her lack of education. I suggested children as an occupation, quite forgetting that no lady need concern herself with anything other than having them. My soul is already in the merchant class. Yes, I like being in trade. It is better to do something with one's life, even if that something is only running a hotel. But I thank you for your offer.'

'I also owe you an apology,' he said. 'I had the temerity to suggest obliquely that you might become my mistress. Am I forgiven?'

She smiled at him suddenly and his heart turned over.

Then, to his fury, Lady Stanton came up to them and sat down.

'Lady Stanton,' said the duke, 'may I be of some assistance to you?' His voice was as cold as ice.

'I wish to be introduced to this charming lady,' said Lady Stanton.

'Of course you do,' said the duke lightly. 'Such beauty always excites admiration and curiosity. But, alas, we must leave you. Our dance, I think.'

Lady Stanton watched them go, her eyes narrowing in fury. Who was this unknown charmer who was spoiling her evening and her chances so effectively? She had asked Lady Darkwood, who had looked flustered and murmured something about 'just a friend' before escaping, and now Rowcester was obviously going out of his way not to introduce her.

Lady Stanton thought hard. Perhaps she is pockmarked under that mask. Or perhaps, she thought with increasing fury, Rowcester has chosen to bring some member of the demi-monde to my ball, and Susan Darkwood has connived at it because she is silly.

The ball was becoming rowdy. Masked balls always were. Some of the men were very drunk. Harriet was dancing the Sir Roger de Coverley with the duke. She noticed Lady Stanton had gone up to the gallery over the ballroom where the orchestra was playing and was staring down at her.

'I should leave,' she whispered urgently to the duke. 'Lady Stanton has become over-curious as to my identity.'

'Let her be curious,' he said with a laugh, and then the dance separated them again.

But when the dance finished, Lady Stanton's voice could be heard calling for silence.

'My friends,' she cried, 'the moment of unmasking is here.'

Laughter all round. Men and women were untying the strings of their masks. The duke slipped his into his pocket and whispered to Harriet, 'Faint!'

She closed her eyes and slid towards the floor. He caught her up in his arms and strode from the room with her while Susan let out an audible gasp of relief.

Still holding her, the duke ran down the stairs. The hall was empty. The footmen who had supplied the guard of honour on arrival were now on duty in the ballroom and supper room, apart from three who were talking to the coachmen outside. The duke opened the nearest door leading off the hall and slipped inside, put Harriet on her feet and, turning round, locked them in.

'Lady Stanton's library, I presume,' said the duke, looking around. Glass cases of books bought by the yard for appearance rather than content ranged the walls. The room had a musty smell and was probably little used.

'Now what?' asked Harriet anxiously.

'Now we wait a few moments in the hope that Lady Stanton will believe we have left. Then I will leave you here and slip out and tell a footman to have my carriage brought forward. It is some way down the street.'

'Oh, thank you,' said Harriet. 'Lady Darkwood would indeed be in deep disgrace were my identity to become known.'

'Let us hope she remains aware of that, otherwise she will gossip. I will go now. When the carriage is ready, I will knock twice on the door.'

'My cloak,' protested Harriet. 'It is in the dressing room.'

'I shall fetch it.'

He unlocked the door and looked out. Then he went out into the hall and Harriet locked the door behind him. She felt nervous and at the same time elated.

When a double knock sounded on the door, she started in alarm, then remembered his signal and cautiously opened it.

'Quickly,' he said. 'Put on your cloak. Now I must pick you up again so that, should we be seen, I can protest that you are still unwell.'

Harriet closed her eyes and felt strong arms lift her up, felt herself pressed against his chest.

He carried her out just as his coach drew up

outside the house. 'Now we are safe,' he said as they moved off. 'You may open your eyes and remove your mask.'

He leaned forward and untied the strings of her mask and dropped it in her lap. The carriage lurched in and out of a hole in the road and she was thrown against him.

She tried to struggle back, but the steadying arm he had put around her tightened. She saw his lips descending, and instead of pushing him away, she closed her eyes again. His lips were warm and urgent, passion rising in him as he remembered that scene in the kitchen. She was responding to him, fuelling his ardour, and his kiss deepened and his long hands caressed her face. He finally drew back with a ragged sigh. 'Oh, Harriet,' he said, 'you bewitch me. When I saw you naked in the kitchen, I thought of Venus rising from the foam.'

Her face went rigid with shock and she shrank back, her eyes wide. Then she blushed, a deep red, painful blush which he could see clearly in the jogging light of the carriage lamp. Then her hands stole up to hide her face.

'I should not have said that.' The duke looked at her wretchedly. 'I went down to the kitchen to talk . . . to talk to you . . . and I saw . . . I saw . . .'

'No more, if you please,' said Harriet, lowering her hands and now as pale as she had been scarlet a moment before. She looked out of the carriage window and saw with relief that they were drawing up outside the hotel.

'Your grace,' she said, 'I have had to be father and mother to myself for quite some time. I have had to be my own chaperone. I do not blame you for kissing me. I did not repulse you. But I will never be able to look at you again without disgust and embarrassment.'

The footman opened the door and then drew back startled as Harriet leaped out past him before he had time to let down the steps.

The duke gloomily told his coachman to take him back to the ball. He had not behaved like a gentleman. The fact that he had seen Harriet naked and had admitted it would never be forgiven or forgotten by her. Old Lord Plomley at the club, who had sired fifteen children, had once confessed in his cups that he had never seen his wife naked, all the rites of the marriage bed having been performed in the pitch-black and under cover of several blankets. 'But that's the way of the world,' the old man had sighed. 'Only tarts take their clothes off.'

SIX

Be good, sweet maid, and let who will be clever.

CHARLES KINGSLEY

Harriet had had permission from the others to stay in bed on the following day, a bed she shared with Miss Tonks and Mrs Budley, accommodation in the attics being cramped.

She felt, rather than saw, them rise, heard the quiet murmur of their voices and the splashing of water from the wash-stand. Then the door opened and closed and she was left alone. She stretched out and tried to go back to sleep, but the sound of the bells would not let her. She was often amazed to hear people talk about the genteel quietness of the West End.

From outside came the usual daily cacophony of bells: bells sounded by hawkers of cheap penknives, ribbons and hot pies; by strolling players, the Punch and Judy man, the ballad singers; by the milkmen and milkmaids, the butcher, the baker, the grocer; by the vendors of fresh spring water, quack medicines and charms; by the beadle, the town crier, the scavenger pushing his cart – all jangled bells of various hideousness. Then there were the bells from the street markets, which rang at seven in the morning, when they opened, and then for half an hour in the evening, when they closed. The church bell-ringers practised peals at all hours. There had been many letters in the newspapers demanding that the government do something to abate the hellish noise.

Sleep would not come and Harriet was almost glad when Miss Tonks crept back in and whispered that Lady Darkwood wished to speak to her.

Harriet was surprised that Susan should rise any time before two in the afternoon, as she glanced at the clock and saw it was only eight-thirty in the morning. She washed and dressed and made her way down to Susan's rooms.

The reason for Susan's being awake was explained by the fact she was still in her ballgown and had obviously not been to bed.

She drew Harriet into the sitting room. 'Talk quietly,' whispered Susan, 'for Darkwood is still asleep next door and does not know how late I returned.'

'Then it would be wise to change into your night-rail and pretend I had roused you should he awake,' said Harriet practically.

'How clever you are!' exclaimed Susan. 'But, then, you are so well-versed in the ways of affairs, and I am not!' And before Harriet could think of any reply to that, she had vanished into the bedroom.

After a short time, she reappeared in a nightgown

and wrapper, her eyes dancing. 'Such larks,' she cried. 'When Rowcester returned to the ball, La Stanton all but fell on his neck, demanding to know the name of his fair inamorata. Quick as a flash, Rowcester says in a freezing voice that the lady was his *cousin*, and Lady Stanton is suddenly all pretty apologies. You must have hatched it up between you. My dear Harriet, I should have guessed that Rowcester was your . . . er hum . . . for he was not going to go to the ball until he heard you were to be there. And Lady Stanton would never have become so suspicious had you not decided to take supper with him.'

'Susan,' said Harriet sternly, 'there is no "er hum" or whatever you like to call it between Rowcester and myself. He was quick-witted enough to rescue me, and you, from an embarrassing disclosure. If he was so enamoured of me, I wager he would not have returned me home and gone back immediately. I am sure he then proceeded to flirt with Lady Stanton.'

'Yes, he did,' said Susan, surprised. 'That is exactly what he did and she looked like the cat with the cream bowl.'

'Philanderer! Rake!' cried outraged voices in Harriet's head. That he should have seen her *naked*, that he should have kissed her, and that she should have responded – all that was disgraceful.

'But it was quite a jolly affair, although Captain Jenners trod on the hem of my gown,' Susan rattled on. 'He apologized so prettily and begged leave to call on me today. So delightful that Darkwood has to

120

go to the House, for he would sit about and huff and puff and spread gloom all over the place.'

'Where are your children?' asked Harriet. 'Asleep?'

'I sent them off to the country with their nurse-maid,' said Susan. 'One never sees them at home, you know, but in the rather cramped quarters of this hotel, they are apt to get underfoot. Silly little things, they cried dreadfully. The country will seem very flat after London.'

'Perhaps they were crying because they were leaving you,' Harriet pointed out.

Susan looked surprised. 'They are very well brought up,' she said severely, 'and not given to any excess of sentimentality, I assure you. Now I must get some sleep so that I will look my best for Captain Jenners.'

Harriet left, wondering if she herself could be such a cold mother, and yet such detachment was expected of anyone in the ranks of society. She made her way downstairs to the hotel office, hoping to find Lady Fortescue, suddenly feeling in need of some comfort and advice.

Lady Fortescue looked up in relief as Harriet entered. 'I cannot make head nor tail of these accounts,' she said. 'Do we have to have beeswax candles? Such an expense.'

'I am afraid so.' Harriet sat down next to her at the desk. 'Tallow ones do smell so. Oil lamps are lit at night now for the guests coming home, but we must make sure they are properly trimmed at all times. A smoking oil lamp can be quite destructive. Do not worry. I awoke early and am now prepared to put the accounts in order.' She hesitated and then said, 'Lady Fortescue, I am in need of advice.'

'Something happened at the ball?' Lady Fortescue's black eyes snapped with curiosity.

'I will try to tell you all without blushing, but I fear it will be hard.' In a halting voice, Harriet told her of the duke's rescuing her from exposure at the ball, the subsequent kiss and the revelation that he had seen her naked in the kitchen.

'You were naked *all over*?'

'Yes, Lady Fortescue,' said Harriet drily, 'that is how one bathes.'

'No, it is not! If you must adopt modern ideas and wash all over, then wear a shift. Horrifying that any man should see you thus, and almost quite as bad that you should see yourself. Well, the damage is done and a lecture on morals will not help. It is quite clear he is enamoured of you, but in a low kind of way. Let me think.'

She rang the handbell on the desk and when a footman answered its summons, told him to fetch Sir Philip.

'Never say you are going to tell Sir Philip what I have just told you,' cried Harriet.

'No, he is too old, and such revelations would excite the old lecher too much. Nonetheless, he is very worldly, and being a horrible satyr, should know the best way to dampen my nephew's ardour. Ah, Sir Philip, the benefit of your wisdom, if you will.'

Sir Philip bent over Lady Fortescue's hand and deposited a moist kiss on the back of it, then leered into her eyes.

'Behave yourself, sir,' said Lady Fortescue, snatching her hand away. 'Here is the problem. Rowcester is still in pursuit of Miss James and with the basest of intentions. What do you suggest? Until the end of the Season, we will not have enough to afford to send her away, and besides, no one can make out the accounts as she can.'

'Speaking of accounts,' said Harriet, 'I do not see any payments to the Sun Insurance Company entered in the books, and that is your department, Sir Philip. You have paid them, have you not?'

'I have indeed, fair lady. Give me the books and I will enter the payments on the appropriate dates. I have it all here,' he said, taking a crumpled piece of paper out of his pocket. 'But you were asking about Rowcester. Let me think. He stays on now, not to ruin us or buy us out, but because of you, Miss James. All he gets is tantalizingly brief glimpses of you, and so you are neither fish nor fowl, neither servant nor respectable member of society. Since you cannot any longer be a respectable member of society' – Harriet winced – 'then you must appear more the servant here to establish your position firmly in his mind. I suggest you begin by waiting table in the dining room.'

'But then he will see me,' exclaimed Harriet.

'In a menial but respectable position,' pointed out Sir Philip.

Harriet thought about that. It would perhaps be for the best. She could show him by the very formality of her manners that she was indeed nothing more than a servant. In front of the other guests, and Lady Fortescue and Colonel Sandhurst, she would be unapproachable.

'I'll do it,' she said.

Colonel Sandhurst came into the office. 'Good morning,' he said, looking brightly about. 'Problems?'

'I was just asking Sir Philip his advice,' began Lady Fortescue, and then wished she had not spoken, for the colonel's face darkened.

'Oh, you were, were you?' he snapped. 'And why was I not consulted?'

Harriet picked up the accounts books and escaped with them up to the schoolroom. Dinner was not served until the new fashionable hour of seven, and so she had plenty of time to go through the accounts.

The grocery bill was still too high. She went down to the kitchen to see Despard, glad that she had been taught sufficient French in the past to be able to communicate with the man. Patiently she explained again that they had to be careful. Although the fashionable grocers, fishmongers and butchers were prepared to allow unlimited credit at the moment, their prices were higher than that of the markets. For economy's sake, it was necessary to spend some hard cash from time to time. She herself would take him round the markets on the following morning and he would see for himself that it was cheaper and better

124

to buy goods there. He listened politely, his twisted face impassive, but Harriet had the feeling she had had before that he did not like her, did not like any of them. Sir Philip for some reason had assumed that Despard, having been pressed into the French army, did not sympathize with Napoleon, Sir Philip having a rare genius for believing what suited his own ends. The only thing that seemed to rouse the French chef to any sort of animation was the new closed stove, which he insisted on cleaning and blackleading himself. Harriet firmly repeated her offer to take him to the markets, saying she would hire a carriage for the purpose and meet him outside the hotel at six in the morning.

She was kept busy that day, for Lady Fortescue and Colonel Sandhurst had decided to settle their differences by going for a walk in the Park, Sir Phlip had disappeared off to wherever he usually disappeared, and Miss Tonks and Mrs Budley had gone to look at the shops. Harriet thought impatiently that the poor relations had got into the way of talking about how hard they worked, while leaving most of it to the hotel servants.

Viscount Chiswick and his lady, guests at the hotel, summoned Harriet to their sitting room. They said they had a serious complaint. There was little in the dining room that they could eat.

'But our cooking is said to be the finest in London,' protested Harriet. Lady Chiswick, a faded woman in her thirties with a querulous voice, pointed out earnestly that neither of them could eat anything with sugar in it, nor could they drink tea, coffee or chocolate.

'Why not?' asked Harriet patiently.

'Because such items are the result of slave labour,' said Lady Chiswick. 'If everyone in England refused to touch such items, then this dreadful trade might diminish.'

Harriet gave a little sigh. It was hard to disagree with such humanitarian motives, but a perpetual effort to balance the books was apt to make one selfish. She took out a notebook she always carried with her. 'Let me see. I could go to the herbalist and get some dandelion root and make coffee from that and use honey to sweeten it.'

'Excellent,' said Lady Chiswick. 'But the food is spiced, and spices come from the West Indies, and so . . .'

'Special dishes will be made for you without spices,' said Harriet, 'but,' she added, 'commendable as your motives are, I must charge you extra for the preparation of these dishes.'

'Nothing is too great an expense where my wife's principles are concerned,' said the viscount.

Harriet went down to the kitchen to tell Despard that he must now prepare special dishes for the Chiswicks, making sure no product of slave labour tainted them.

His face looked more twisted than ever. 'We got rid of such effete parasites in France,' he remarked caustically in French.

'We do not yet have the guillotine here,' snapped

Harriet, and went back upstairs to get dressed and walk to the City to buy dandelion root.

The day seemed to rush past and on her return she only just had time to change into the formal black silk gown and white apron and cap that Lady Fortescue considered correct apparel for waiting table.

Harriet found it less of an ordeal than she had expected. The duke was not present, and after a few curious looks thrown in her direction by the diners, they settled down to treating her like any other servant: that is, they ignored her completely, most of them noticing only the white-gloved hands which deftly slid the dishes under their noses.

But the Chiswicks spoke to her on leaving the dining room, praising the efforts made on their behalf, which all went to show, thought Harriet, that high-principled people appeared to have charming manners as well.

Lady Stanton had a few beaux which she kept dancing attendance on her. One of them, Mr Jasper Blackley, was selected to find her something amusing the following evening when she found the only choice was a programme of German lieder at the home of old Lady Rumbelow.

Mr Blackley was only too anxious to please. 'There is that new hotel everyone is talking about – The Poor Relation.'

Lady Stanton smiled at him. 'How clever of you. That is where Rowcester is living at the moment, is it not?'

'I had forgot that,' said Mr Blackley gloomily. 'There is always the opera.'

'Perhaps later. I have a mind to dine at this new hotel.'

'I believe it is very difficult to get a table,' commented Mr Blackley, and then shrank a little before the impatient gleam in Lady Stanton's eyes.

'I am sure you can find a table if you really put your mind to it,' said Lady Stanton in a caressing voice, which nonetheless held the required amount of threat.

So Mr Blackley contrived to get a table by dint of bribing Sir Philip Sommerville, who was acting as maître d'hôtel and had already made a comfortable sum out of such bribes which he did not trouble to put into the general kitty. Sir Philip seemed to have an instinct that told him at precisely what time some hopeful diner would appear at the hotel demanding a table, for although often absent earlier in the day, he was always there later on to handle any bookings.

When Harriet saw Lady Stanton walk in, her heart sank and yet she was glad that Rowcester had obviously chosen to be absent from the dining room that evening as well.

Lady Stanton looked about her, amused to notice Lady Fortescue and Colonel Sandhurst, of whom she had heard, creaking round the tables with the dishes. Clever of them, too, to have such a pretty waitress. But there was something familiar about that waitress. That black hair and those green eyes. She could almost be that masked charmer at her ball, but could not, of course, be, for had not Rowcester said she was his cousin?

To her delight, the duke himself walked in. Wishing Mr Blackley at the devil, Lady Stanton smiled at the duke. He stooped to kiss her hand and then seemed to freeze. Startled, Lady Stanton looked up at him and noticed he was staring beyond her.

She tried to twist round to see who or what it was that had caught his attention, but he held fast to her hand and said, 'How wonderful to see you again.'

'You did not call on me after the ball to pay your respects,' chided Lady Stanton.

'I sent my servant.'

'Not at all the same thing, as well you know. Do join us, Rowcester.'

'I would not interfere in your tête-à-tête for the world.'

'Do not let Mr Blackley worry you. He is merely an old friend of the family. *You* want Rowcester to join us, do you not, Jasper?'

'If you wish,' said Mr Blackley sulkily.

'Alas,' said the duke, 'I see my own table is ready for me.'

He bowed and left. Lady Stanton made a disappointed grimace.

Harriet was pleased to notice that her hands were quite steady as she ladled out a bowl of white soup made from veal and ground almonds and placed it in front of the duke.

'Is this some kind of joke?' he demanded angrily.

'On the contrary, your grace,' said Harriet smoothly, 'you will find the soup excellent.'

Lady Stanton with narrowed eyes noticed the exchange, although she could not hear what was being said.

And then Susan came in on the arm of her husband. 'Why, Harriet, what are you doing here?' she demanded in a loud voice.

'I work here,' said Harriet.

'Don't speak in that familiar way to the servants,' said her husband with a scowl.

'But it isn't a servant, light of my life,' pouted Susan. 'It's Harriet.'

'Would you hail a member of the demi-monde as a servant?' demanded Lord Darkwood loudly. 'No! You wouldn't. And any lady of quality who sinks to waiting on table is worse than a trollop on the streets, mark my words.'

'Evening, Darkwood,' said the duke, 'I heard your speech in the House of Lords.'

'What did you think, hey? Blistering stuff.'

'On the contrary,' said the duke evenly, 'it was the most dreadful, boring fustian I have ever listened to in my life.'

'You forget yourself. I have a good mind to call you out.'

'Do that,' said the duke with a sweet smile.

'You there!' Lady Stanton summoned Harriet with an imperious wave. 'This soup is cold.'

'Demme, of course it's cold,' snarled Mr Blackley, who was out of charity with her. 'You've been sitting over it this age.'

Lady Fortescue caught Harriet's arm as she was

about to go to Lady Stanton. 'Get Sir Philip,' she whispered.

Harriet found Sir Philip asleep in the office, a bottle of burgundy in front of him. She shook the old man awake and explained rapidly that Lady Stanton was being 'difficult'.

Sir Philip headed rapidly for the dining room with his odd crablike scuttle.

Lady Fortescue was standing over Lady Stanton, who was saying, 'You may be playing by pretending to run a hotel, but with the prices you charge, you should at least try to make sure the soup is hot.'

Sir Philip rushed up. Lady Fortescue, with a smile on her thin rouged lips, stood back.

'Complaining about the prices, hey?' he said in a loud voice. 'If you cannot pay, my lady, then I must ask you to leave a piece of jewellery as security.'

The sheer effrontery of the remark left Lady Stanton speechless for once in her life.

'My lady was merely saying the soup was cold, not complaining about the charge,' snapped Mr Black-ley.

Sir Philip picked up Lady Stanton's plate of soup, carried it to the sideboard, ladled more soup into another dish from the tureen, which was being kept warm over a spirit burner, and carried it back.

'There you are,' he said. 'Anything else?'

'The soup really is excellent,' said the duke, his clear voice carrying round the dining room.

'What would you know about soup, or anything else for that matter?' raged Lord Darkwood. 'A man who cannot appreciate one of the best speeches the Lords has ever heard cannot appreciate anything.'

'A man who insults a gently born lady in public is a churl,' retorted the duke venomously.

'Oh, do stop them,' whispered Lady Fortescue urgently to Sir Philip.

'Do you know, I don't think I will,' said Sir Philip gleefully. 'This will be all over Town tomorrow and will add to our consequence. I insulted Lady Stanton, and the duke and Darkwood are arguing publicly over one of the servants.'

'But no one will come if they think they are going to be insulted by an old fright like you,' said the colonel nastily.

''Course they will. The upper classes have a masochistic streak and fawn on anyone who insults them. How do you think Beau Brummell became so popular? Give it a few moments and Darkwood will be crawling to the duke.'

Lord Darkwood sat in a moody silence. He had visions of the duke, who was a maliciously witty orator, attacking him in the House of Lords and making him look like a fool. Besides, this wretched waitress was a friend of his wife, and *she* was looking daggers at him as if rehearsing the scene she was going to enjoy making as soon as they were in private.

He threw down his napkin – a newfangled sophistry which puzzled some of the diners, who still wiped their mouths on the tablecloth – and crossed to the duke's table.

He sat down opposite and said in a conciliatory voice, 'We are becoming overhasty. I am sorry I appeared to insult Miss James.'

'And I am sorry I criticized your speech,' said the duke with a sudden charming smile. 'I was, in fact, most impressed.'

'Well, now,' said Lord Darkwood, elated with relief, 'I must say it is indeed a pity that Miss James there should lower herself to wait on table.'

'Miss James is very competent, but I sometimes think it must be a very dreary life for her. She has no amusements or pleasures.'

So the duke was interested in making Miss James his mistress, thought Darkwood. What other interest could he have in a female who had sunk so low? If he, Darkwood, helped the duke with his ambition, then he was sure he would have the duke's undying gratitude, not to mention his considerable influence at court.

'Come to think of it,' he said, 'I haven't been taking my poor wife about much. She has a desire to go to Vauxhall. Rowdy place, but that sort of thing amuses her. Perhaps I could beg you to be of our party tomorrow night, say. I am sure my wife would be delighted if Miss James joined us.'

The duke thought briefly of telling him to go to the devil. He did not like his interest in Harriet being pointed out in this obvious way. But he would have an opportunity to apologize to her properly. 'I would like that. Thank you,' he said. 'May I suggest your lady asks Miss James but does not say I am to be of the party?'

'Gladly.'

Lady Stanton strained her ears and managed to pick up 'Vauxhall' and 'tomorrow night'. She turned to her escort. 'I have a mind to go to Vauxhall tomorrow night,' she said.

'If you will,' said Mr Blackley discourteously, for he had not forgiven her for making a scene.

Harriet had been sent out of the dining room for, as Lady Fortescue said, 'If her very presence is going to start gentlemen challenging each other to duels, then she is better out of the way.'

Harriet was summoned by Susan later that evening and found to her surprise that Susan's husband was also there and making a supreme effort to appear cordial.

'Darkwood has just had the most marvellous idea,' said Susan. 'He is taking us to Vauxhall tomorrow evening. Please say you will come. Such fun!'

'Yes, indeed,' said Lord Darkwood. 'Apologize for any comments you may have overheard in the dining room, Miss James, but distress at your situation prompted some ill-chosen remarks. Please forgive me.'

'There! He's apologized like the lambkin he is,' said Susan, 'so you cannot refuse, Harriet. Too churlish. We shall quiz all the gowns and have such larks!'

It was the duke who had changed Darkwood's mind, thought Harriet. Would he be there? But Susan would have said so. But then Susan had said that the duke would not be at the ball. Perhaps he would be there, so what was the point in her going? He wanted her as his mistress, and no man in love would offer her such a degrading situation. But *if* she went and *if* he were there, she could demonstrate to him exactly how little he meant to her.

'Thank you, Lord Darkwood,' she said. 'I accept your apology and your kind invitation.'

The poor relations breakfasted in the schoolroom the next morning as usual, served by John and Betty. Harriet, tired after her early-morning expedition to the markets, often wondered what Lady Fortescue's old servants thought of the arrangement because they were always correct, never letting any of their thoughts show on their faces. Lady Fortescue had expressed a wish to buy them a cottage somewhere as soon as they were in funds, to which John and Betty had said a polite thank-you, but almost as if they thought such a great day would never arrive.

A page-boy scratched at the door and entered. 'Beg parding,' he said, 'but there's a Mrs Blessop downstairs what wants to know if the Miss Letitia Tonks what is a partner here is her sister.'

Miss Tonks let out a squawk of dismay and then cried, 'What shall I do? She will berate me, bully me, might even cut off my little allowance. I cannot face her.'

'Tell her Miss Tonks will be down in a minute,' said Sir Philip, and the page went off.

'How could you?' demanded Miss Tonks, wringing her hands.

'Stow your whids,' jeered Sir Philip. 'She wants a

Miss Tonks, she'll get a Miss Tonks. I need a dress and bonnet.'

Lady Fortescue's black eyes gleamed with laughter. 'Never say, Sir Philip, that you are going to masquerade as Miss Tonks!'

'Exactly. Now I'm a little fellow, so it'd better be one of your gowns, Mrs Budley.'

Mrs Budley gloomily thought of which of her gowns she should sacrifice, for after it had been hung on Sir Philip's unlovely body, she had no intention of ever wearing it again. She then thought of a plain puce gown she had never liked, and her face brightened. Also, there was a bonnet like a coal-scuttle which she knew did not become her.

Soon Sir Philip, suitably attired, made his way down the stairs to the coffee room, where a footman told him Mr and Mrs Blessop were waiting.

Sir Philip stood in the doorway and studied Miss Tonks's sister and decided he did not like what he saw. Where Miss Tonks was vague-looking and sheepish, this woman was hard, with a great slab of a face and squiggly black teeth. Her body was so rigidly corseted that she looked like a solid tube with a head stuck on top of it.

'You wanted to see me?' asked Sir Philip, approaching slowly.

'*You* are Miss Tonks?' said Mrs Blessop, looking him up and down.

'Yes, yes, yes. Evidently, yes. Told you it was all a mistake,' babbled her husband, a rabbity-looking man in a high collar.

'I am Miss Tonks,' said Sir Philip, beginning to enjoy himself. 'What is your business with me? If you wish to reside here, I am afraid I must refuse. We are very particular about our guests.'

'I would not reside here if you paid me to,' said Mrs Blessop waspishly.

'Then stop wasting my time and clear off,' retorted Sir Philip gleefully.

Mrs Blessop rose to her feet with a massive creak of corsets. She sounded like a square-rigger in a chopping gale. 'I was under the false impression that my sister had had the folly to lend her name to this low enterprise. Good day to you, madam.'

'And good day to you, you old . . .' Sir Philip used a four-letter word which began with *c*. Neither Mr or Mrs Blessop could believe their ears.

But one look at this ugly old 'woman's' face persuaded both of them that if they stayed and challenged her, worse might be to come.

Sir Philip grinned as they marched off. He felt elated and his faded old eyes ranged round the coffee room looking for more mischief. A Bond Street Lounger was sitting reading a newspaper, his feet up on the table.

Sir Philip sat down next to him. 'Morning, my fair charmer,' he leered. 'What about a big smacking kiss?'

Harriet spent that day altering one of her old gowns and embellishing it with the green silk ribbons picked off the ballgown. Lady Fortescue had given her permission to go, saying indulgently that although Lady Darkwood was a silly rattle, she had a good heart, and Darkwood had evidently apologized nicely for his insults. Privately Lady Fortescue hoped that if Harriet went about socially, she might meet some man who was prepared to marry her despite her lack of dowry. Such things did occasionally happen. Such a beautiful, capable girl, thought Lady Fortescue. She would make some clergyman, say, a good wife.

Setting out in the Darkwoods' carriage with no sign of the duke in sight made Harriet almost forget all the grand speeches she had been rehearsing and settle back to enjoy an uncomplicated evening.

Lord Darkwood, made indulgent by the prospect of political help from the duke, had the carriage stop on Westminster Bridge, where they alighted to look at the view.

It was a warm evening, with a pale green sky. The view was magnificent, the curve of the river to Somerset House and St Paul's very fine, the glittering bosom of the stream covered by barges, sailboats and watermen's wherries, skimming about like dragonflies on a pond. The wherrymen and sailors were all singing, and more music came from a merry party setting off by boat to Vauxhall, and another party amusing themselves by blowing French horns under the arches of the bridge to awaken strange echoes. The air was charged with excitement, that restless feeling that London always had as its thousands set out to drink and gamble and dance, a devil-take-tomorrow feeling, all too understandable in an age when death daily stalked the streets in the guise of every plague and illness, from cholera to smallpox.

Harriet felt a tinge of sadness as she watched the river turning silver in the twilight and heard the music and laughter. She felt very old. Twenty-eight was a great age, an age to put on caps and forget about marriage.

She was quite subdued by the time they reached Vauxhall, and thought all her planned speeches to the duke silly. She was in trade, and had therefore put herself into the position where she must marry someone else in trade or stay a spinster.

Vauxhall was crowded, gaily dressed men and women strolling up and down the long alleys under the trees. Harriet was in a composed frame of mind as they approached the boxes near where the band in its cockle-shell stand was playing music. She must enjoy this evening because such an evening would possibly never occur again. And then, as they climbed up to the box which Lord Darkwood had reserved, she saw the duke waiting for them and looked wide-eyed at Susan.

'He is so handsome,' said Susan, 'and besides, what can he do when you are chaperoned by me?'

Thinking bleakly that Susan was possibly the least careful of chaperones anyone could possibly have, Harriet curtsied to the duke, thought of his remarks about seeing her naked and blushed painfully, and then sat down at the table with her head averted and tried to concentrate on the music.

'Now, *isn't* this pleasant,' crowed Susan, although her voice came out in a suffocated way. Susan had not been aware of the discoloration of her own teeth until faced with the pure whiteness of Harriet's, and had tried to develop a manner of speaking which would not let them show. She was wearing a gown of white velvet striped with bands of white silk and cut very low to show a generous bosom painted with white lead, for Susan had freckles on her bosom which she thought unfair of the gods to inflict on her. Her face and arms were also painted with white lead so that she looked like a tall and amiable ghost.

Harriet's gown was of plain brown silk, bought when she had been trying to obtain a post as a governess. Although it now sported the green silk ribbons and shoulder bows from the ballgown, she felt dowdy and wished she had some jewellery. Susan was wearing a diamond tiara on her head and a great collar of diamonds around her neck. She had diamond bracelets over her white gloves. If I had one of those bracelets, Harriet found herself thinking covetously, I could set myself up for life. But that thought was followed closely by another. What was it that Sir Philip had stolen from the duke which had given enough money to pay the builders and decorators for the new hotel? Could it be a piece of jewellery? But jewellery did not fetch the price it once did, because of all the French emigrants resident in London who were selling their jewels off. Not unless it had been something magnificent.

'You are dreaming, Miss James,' said the duke.

'I was listening to the music,' replied Harriet.

'Then you can *both* listen to the music,' said Susan gaily. 'Come, Darkwood, I have a mind to see the hermit.'

'But Susan . . .' Harriet began to protest, but Susan was already making her way down the stairs, with her oddly complacent husband behind her.

After a little silence, the duke said gently, 'I offer you my most humble apology for the embarrassment I caused you the other night, Miss James. Pray say you will forgive me so that we may be comfortable again.'

Harriet looked at him doubtfully. 'Your grace, I have no parents to ask you your intentions. I have no wish to become your mistress.'

'Friendship,' he said. 'Shall we agree on friendship?'

'Gladly.' Harriet smiled on him charmingly and gave him her hand, which he shook, although he had to restrain himself from raising it to his lips.

'I see Lady Stanton has just arrived,' he observed, 'and has not yet seen us, so perhaps we should take a stroll.'

'Naturally you cannot be seen with a waitress,' said Harriet.

'Naturally not,' he replied gravely, 'or you would indeed be damned as my mistress. Were the Darkwoods here with us, then that would be another

141

matter. I have seen no one, other than Lady Stanton and her escort, who was in the dining room last night. I suggest we go to find the Darkwoods so that we may all return together and be comfortable.'

Harriet took his offered arm once they were in the walk. At least he had wanted to escape Lady Stanton, she thought with a lightness of heart. They promenaded through the alleys, stopped to hear Mrs Mountain sing 'Home, Again', a popular ballad. The tender music throbbed on the soft air and hushed the revellers. Then they moved on to admire the tin waterfall and so towards the fireworks display.

The crowd swayed backwards and forwards and oohed and aahed as each burst of stars hit the night sky. Harriet was pressed close against the duke's side, hardly able to watch the tumultuous tumbling firework stars in the sky for the tumult of emotions inside her.

She did not know whether to be glad or sorry when the display finished and they walked back sedately down the walk.

'I do believe Mrs Mountain is being asked for an encore,' said the duke. 'Would you like to hear her again? The Darkwoods are not yet back in the box.'

Harriet nodded. Mrs Mountain was being called on to sing 'Home, Again' once more. Harriet listened to the words this time, and sentimental as they were, they suddenly gave her a lost feeling, and started her wondering if she herself would ever have a proper home again.

The evening light is failing fast,
The birds have gone to rest.
And, oh, that I were home again,
Safe in my family's breast.

The last note trailed away, and then the applause was deafening. Harriet surreptitiously wiped away her tears. She had had a poignant memory of sitting beside the fire on a dark winter's evening writing careful letters on a slate for her governess while her mother sewed and her father read.

'You are crying,' said the duke quickly.

'I am over-sentimental,' said Harriet. 'I see the Darkwoods are returned.'

The duke silently damned the Darkwoods. He realized he had been hoping to guide her along one of the darker walks and steal a kiss. But he had offered her friendship.

And then he began to think: of course, I could marry her. The thought was outrageous, but still . . . He owed a lot to his family name, but yet . . . There were all those long years of fending off matchmaking mothers, counter-jumpers, mushrooms and toadies of every description. He had armoured himself in pride. He had become expert at keeping the pretentious and encroaching at bay. It was too bad that Harriet should have chosen such a vulgar profession. Had she joined the ranks of the demi-monde, then he could have made her his mistress. But raging passions and lusts apart, he wanted more from her than that. I want, he thought gloomily, her very soul.

She has bewitched me; she is like a poison in my blood, seeping through my body until my wits are lost.

Arrogance warred with longing so that by the time they reached the box, the normally urbane and self-possessed duke replied abstractedly to Susan's banter and did not even protest when Lady Stanton, with Mr Blackley in tow, insisted on joining them. Susan chattered, Lady Stanton flirted with the duke, Mr Blackley politely talked about the state of the nation to Lord Darkwood while Harriet sat with her hands clenched in her lap, staring straight ahead, and the duke drank glass after glass of rack punch and did not seem to hear what anyone was saying to him until Lady Stanton penetrated his thoughts by remarking loudly in a voice edged with pique, 'So bold of you to bring that serving maid out with you, Rowcester.'

'If you mean Miss James, say so,' he snapped. 'Miss James is a friend of mine.'

'Really?' Lady Stanton, her eyes on those green bows, was now sure who her masked rival at the ball had been. 'I thought she was your cousin.'

'Lady Stanton, I beg you to excuse us,' said the duke, rising to his feet, 'but Miss James is fatigued and must return home.'

'Miss James is not fatigued,' said Harriet quickly. 'Pray be seated, your grace.'

'I was only trying to protect you from further insult,' protested the duke.

'From Lady Stanton?' said Harriet, slowly uncurl-

144

ing her claws. 'No one, least of all me, pays any attention to the remarks of the vulgar.'

'Oh, bravo, Harriet,' said Susan, clapping her hands. 'Do run along, Lady Stanton. I don't want you, Rowcester don't want you, my husband don't want you . . . oh, run along, do. You quite try my patience.'

Lady Stanton rose and made her way to the steps. Then she turned and faced the group. 'You will be sorry you ever crossed me,' she hissed.

Making deprecatory movements with his hands behind her back, Mr Blackley followed her.

'Such a relief to hear you sounding quite human, Harriet,' said Susan cheerfully. 'You are become so prim and proper.'

'It is necessary in my position to stay prim and proper,' said Harriet.

Lord Darkwood threw her a nervous look. If she was going to turn hoity-toity with the duke, it might reflect on his political chances.

'My love,' he said to his wife, 'I crave exercise.'

Susan looked surprised. Lord Darkwood gave her a portentous wink and she coloured and giggled and rose to her feet. 'Come, then,' she said gaily. 'I am sure Miss James and Rowcester wish to be alone.'

'Susan!' exclaimed Harriet desperately, but, giggling and hanging on to her husband's arm, Susan was already leaving the box.

It was then that the duke, glancing out idly over the crowd, saw his widowed mother, the Dowager Duchess of Rowcester, arriving with a small party of friends. His mother, as usual, was painted and rouged and quite drunk. Her escort of slim, effeminate young men were laughing and tittering and posturing about her.

What on earth would Harriet think of such a mother and such companions?

'I think we should follow our friends' example,' he said quickly, 'and take another walk ourselves.'

Harriet went with him with a certain reluctance. She was frightened she might find herself alone with him in one of the dark walks. She did not trust her own feelings. She was conscious of his strength, his virility and of a throbbing excitement emanating from him.

They had just turned a corner of the main alley – the walks were called alleys at Vauxhall – when they saw Lady Stanton with Mr Blackley.

'Quickly,' said the duke, guiding Harriet into one of the darker alleys. 'I have had enough of that pair for one evening.'

Harriet looked around nervously. The alley they were in was so narrow that the trees met overhead, hiding the moon. It was hard to see where one was going. She stumbled and the duke put an arm around her waist to support her.

The feel of her body made his senses reel and he stopped and drew her to him, murmuring, 'Harriet. Oh, my Harriet.'

She should have pushed him away, but her body was fusing and melting hotly into his. Her body was ignoring the directions of her mind. Her lips were raised to his, slightly parted, and when his own came down on hers, the whole of Vauxhall whirled about them and disappeared up into the sky, far above the trees and the lights and music, leaving them locked together in a private world of dark, soft passion.

A drunken couple stumbled into the walk, and Harriet and the duke broke apart and stood staring at each other in a dazed way.

They slowly turned together and started to walk back towards the main alley. But before they reached it, a woman's voice, high and shrill, exclaimed, 'My dear Lady Stanton. Rowcester is enamoured of a serving wench, you say?'

'Oh, yes,' came Lady Stanton's voice. 'And worse than that, Rowcester's own mother is here. I was observing them discreetly, and when he saw his mother he looked quite stricken, for the shame of being seen with such a creature must have hit him, for he rushed her off into the darkness.'

All the lights went out in Harriet's soul. 'Is your mother here?' she asked quietly.

'Yes, but—'

She ran lightly away from him, darting off through the trees. He stood for a moment, surprised, before running after her. But search as he might, there was no sign of Harriet. He returned to the box and waited. Susan and her husband came back, exclaiming at Harriet's absence. They had supper, they drank a great deal of punch, but still Harriet did not appear.

When they all returned to The Poor Relation, the

duke asked the sleepy porter if Miss James had returned. 'Came 'ome in an 'ack two hours ago, your grace,' said the porter.

The duke was at first relieved, and then furious. But whether he was angry with Harriet for having run away, or whether he was furious with himself for mismanaging the whole evening, he did not know.

SEVEN

Perhaps, thought the duke, it was all for the best. He was sitting up in bed, sipping his morning chocolate and reading a letter which had just been handed to him by his servant. In it, Lord Bunbary thanked the duke for his hospitality but regretted that due to his elder daughter's having caught the chicken-pox, they were all forced to retire to the country. In fact, they were leaving that very day.

So, he mused, he would be able to return to his town house, to live surrounded by the dignity that suited his great station in life, to be away from this odd hotel, and most of all, to be away from Harriet James.

He had done enough. He could not spend the rest of his life crawling around after her apologizing for some imagined slight, he told himself. He would regain the calm tenor of his days, free from burning and aching and longing.

He told his valet to ask Sir Philip to present his bill. When the bill arrived, the duke scrutinized it carefully, striking off various additions, such as two bottles of champagne which he had not drunk, and a chamber-pot which he had not broken.

Harriet heard the news of his departure with feelings that she told herself firmly were all ones of relief. A man who fled from his own mother because he was ashamed of the lady he was accompanying was not worth a second thought.

The guests at the hotel had all gone out that afternoon to watch the soldiers drilling in Hyde Park, for the Prince of Wales was to be present, and so the hotel seemed strangely quiet. The day was unusually warm and the malodorous smells of the London streets filtered through even the tightest-closed windows.

Harriet drifted downstairs. There was no longer any fear of meeting the duke. Sir Philip said he had paid his bill correctly, omitting to tell Harriet that the duke had paid exactly what he owed and no more. Harriet entered the money in the accounts book. A healthy sum of money was pouring into the coffers of The Poor Relation. Although many of the guests would not pay their bills until the end of the Season, the money from the dining room and coffee room was an enormous amount. This sign of financial security should have lifted Harriet's spirits, but she felt depressed. How dare Rowcester demean her in such a way and then move out of her range where he could no longer see how she despised him?

And then, despite her bitter thoughts about him, she noticed that there was still no record of the fire insurance having been paid. There were sixteen fire-insurance companies operating in London. Premiums were all surprisingly reasonable, considering the fact that many of the buildings in London were still made of timber and the fire engines were poor, manual affairs.

There was no official fire brigade. Each fire-insurance company had its badge stamped out on sheet lead, painted and gilded, and then nailed on the front of the house or business insured. There was no such badge on the hotel. The last time she had approached Sir Philip on the subject, he had said the insurance company was preparing an extra special badge for them. There were three categories of insurance: common insurance, hazard insurance and the most expensive, doubly hazardous insurance. Sir Philip said he had paid for the doubly hazardous insurance.

She resolved to question Sir Philip on the matter as soon as she could find him.

At that moment, Sir Philip was the subject under discussion by Lady Fortescue and Colonel Sandhurst. They had gone for a walk, but not to Hyde Park, which was full of crowds and noise, but down to St James's Park, which lay under the shadow of Buckingham House, or the Queen's House, as it was more popularly known.

'You run to him the whole time for help and

advice,' the colonel was complaining. 'You never think to turn to me.'

Lady Fortescue sighed. She had been feeling tired of late. She hoped that after all her years of good health she was not going to succumb to any of the wasting illnesses of old age.

'We are running a hotel,' she said brusquely. 'It is a charlatan's job. I am not a charlatan, and neither are you. Sir Philip is. In fact, he is amoral. Would you stoop to any of the low tricks he gets up to? Would you have dressed as a woman and pretended to be Miss Tonks?'

'I feel you often encourage him in a lot of folly,' said the colonel. 'Besides, despite the fact we are still living on our small incomes and taking little out of the hotel funds, Sir Philip contrives to buy something new each week to wear.'

Lady Fortescue looked surprised. 'To tell the truth,' she remarked, 'he's such an ugly little man, I never notice anything he is wearing.'

'Indeed!' The colonel began to feel quite charitable towards Sir Philip. 'Nonetheless,' he went on in a mollified tone of voice, 'there is the question of what he stole from Rowcester. He will never tell anyone. The threat of discovery is hanging over us all. I think we must have been mad. We could all end up in the dock at Newgate.'

'Whatever it was,' said Lady Fortescue slowly, 'Sir Philip seems to have no fear of being found out.'

'The other thing I wished to discuss with you,' went on the colonel, 'is our future.'

'*Our* future?' echoed Lady Fortescue, and threw him a roguish look.

'Yes, all of us,' said the colonel, staring straight ahead and unaware that a bleak frost was now shining in Lady Fortescue's eyes. 'Miss James says everything's looking very healthy. Perhaps we could return the hotel to a home at the end of the year, invest what we have made and live quietly.'

'I have lived quietly for too long,' said Lady Fortescue. 'We are such a success. It is rumoured the Prince of Wales himself will visit us. We are *known*. Our success will continue. Our hitherto drab lives are full of light and colour. We have servants to wait on us. We live, thanks to the hotel, in the style of members of society.'

'Members of society,' commented the colonel drily, 'do not wait table, neither do they have a drawing room in the schoolroom, nor do they have to share cramped bedrooms. It is good of our three ladies to volunteer to share a room and a bed, for it leaves Sir Philip, you and me with our private cubbyholes, but nonetheless . . .'

'Nonetheless you do not seem to be offering any reasonable alternative.' Lady Fortescue stabbed at the unoffending grass viciously with the end of her parasol, a parasol which all too recently in her mind she had been debating whether to sell for food.

The colonel sighed. 'Perhaps I am expecting too much,' he said. His dream had always been that he would once more have enough money to belong to the Cavalry Club and White's, to drive a smart carriage, to wear fine clothes, to talk to what was left of his old army chums on equal social terms. But who was going to greet him on equal social terms after the stigma of trade had firmly attached itself to his name?

Besides, it was all a dream. His old life had been a peculiarly lonely one. When the Season was over and his friends left for the country, there had been no one to go home to in the evenings. He had never married. There had been a woman once, an American, when he had been captured and put on parole outside Boston. She had been a vivacious widow with free and easy manners. After the war with America was over and he was back in England, he had written to her, hoping to return, hoping to marry her, but she had written to say she had married an American officer, and that was that. And most of his friends were dead.

But he did often wish that Sir Philip had not coerced them all into this mad idea of running a hotel. God put one in one's appointed station, and to move out of it was flying in the face of Providence. It might seem ridiculous to the enlightened that an elderly gentleman feared the wrath of God because he had decided to work for a living, but most would have agreed with the colonel, for it was a comforting philosophy which made one able to turn a blind eye to the misery of the paupers on the streets of London. Life was but a journey. The better life lay ahead for everyone when they went home to heaven. People were even hanged on a Friday, the authorities having somehow worked out that it would take them until Sunday morning to get to heaven, and arriving on that holy day would no doubt save their immortal souls.

This day was a Friday, and in the distance sounded the great bell of St Sepulchre's at Newgate, announcing another series of hangings. To a lot of people, a hanging was an excusably jolly affair, where one could wear one's best clothes and eat gingerbread. For were not the wretches on the scaffold going to meet their Maker?

And yet, before he had met Lady Fortescue in the Park, the colonel realized with surprise that he had become reconciled to the idea of death, almost ready to welcome Death himself as a friend.

Now? Well, now he meant to eat and drink sparingly and take gentle exercise, for the days were full of life and colour and companionship.

And so he surprised Lady Fortescue by suddenly seizing her black-mittened hand and kissing it. 'I owe you a lot,' he said.

'You old flirt!' exclaimed Lady Fortescue, highly pleased.

The colonel eyed her slim, erect figure dressed in heavy black and said, 'I often wonder what you would look like in something . . . er, brighter.'

'I have worn mourning for my dead husband these twenty years,' said Lady Fortescue, and then added on a lighter note, 'That all sounds very proper, but the fact is that I had no reason to wear anything else, and new clothes would have cost money. It is still an

155

impossibility but ... Miss James is so very clever with a needle. I wonder if she could trim one of my gowns for me, just to see how it would look.'

And in high good humour with each other, the couple walked on under the trees.

Sir Philip strolled back from the City where he had stood unobserved at the corner of Amen Lane and watched the arrest of Mr Evans, the crook who hired those French wretches out as servants. Sir Philip had sent an anonymous letter to the authorities and then had let justice take its course.

As he walked down Ludgate Hill to the Fleet River, he saw that a building in Farringdon Street was blazing merrily. He felt a pang from his never very active conscience. The money which should have gone to the insurance company he had spent on little knick-knacks for himself: a snuff-box, a new chestnut-brown wig which he had not yet had the courage to wear, and a pair of Hessian boots. Somehow he would need to raise the money to pay the insurance. But perhaps tomorrow ... The thieving of that grand necklace from the duke often worried him. He had only stolen trifles before. And it was not only the necklace, but all the stuff from the attics. If the duke had so quickly noticed those missing candlesticks which Lady Fortescue had tried to take, it surely would not be long before his housekeeper did an inventory of the attics and reported the thefts. But would she? He had never before heard of anyone bothering about what was in the attics of a stately home until the bailiffs called, and they were not likely to call on the rich Duke of Rowcester.

How free and easy he had felt about taking things to ward off starvation. How easy it was to feel guilty now with a good meal in his belly and shillings in his pocket. He moved towards the network of alley-ways which formed that Holborn slum called The Rookery and stopped at a dingy shop just on the outside of the quarter. The shop claimed to sell old clothes, but it was in the back-shop that Virgil Flamand, fence, forger and jeweller, performed his real trade.

'Got anything for me?' asked Virgil. 'I'm busy with this piece of work. All legitimate, too. Diamond necklace for Lady Lesington. She sells the real thing on the quiet to meet her gambling debts, I give her a paste copy, husband never knows, everyone happy.'

'That necklace I sold you,' said Sir Philip, dusting a chair and sitting down. 'I suppose you broke it up.'

Virgil raised his dirty hands to heaven. 'A piece like that? No, I'm waiting till the dust settles before I move it. Think I could sell it on the quiet in one piece.'

'I may pay you a little from time to time to keep it safe until I am in a position to buy it back from you,' Sir Philip found himself saying.

'Turning honest in your old age?'

'Something like that,' said Sir Philip.

'It would suit me,' said Virgil. 'I'll give you time,

and if you don't buy it back, it should be cold enough for me to sell at a good price. Honesty don't suit you, Sir Philip, if you don't mind me saying so.'

'It's an uncomfortable thing, a conscience,' said Sir Philip. 'Ever trouble you, Virgil?'

The jeweller looked amazed. 'I'm a craftsman. Why should my conscience trouble me?'

Feeling comforted now that there was hope the necklace could be reclaimed, Sir Philip went into a chop-house and ordered a plate of mutton washed down with small beer. He would need to tell the others what he had done, and Harriet would need to begin to put by such sums as she could. They wouldn't like it, but they would like the threat of Newgate less.

Mrs Budley and Miss Tonks had gone to watch the troops drilling in Hyde Park. The heat was suffocating and brassy, but both were in high good humour, for a captain had twirled his moustaches at Mrs Budley and Miss Tonks felt sure that the friend with him had eyed *her* in such a speaking way.

'Was it pleasant, being married?' asked Miss Tonks after the crowds had started to disperse and both, reluctant to return, had decided to go for a walk by the Serpentine.

'Oh, so very pleasant,' said Mrs Budley. 'Mr Budley was so gay and charming, and we never seemed to have any worries, apart, that is, from not having children. I would dearly have liked children. But, yes, it was wonderful to have a gentleman to escort one everywhere and not have to worry any more about doing one's duty to one's family. I was very sad when my parents died, but not too sad, for I had Mr Budley to look after me. It is probably just as well I did not know about the debts that were mounting up. Mr Budley used to laugh when the bills came in and tell me not to bother my head about them.'

'I would have liked to marry,' said Miss Tonks wistfully. 'I made such a silly mistake with Mr Blessop, my sister's husband. I was so sure he was courting *me*. And Mama and Papa were sure of it as well. He always stood up with me *twice* at balls and only once with Honoria, my sister. And then . . . and then . . . one ball he did not dance with me at all. He did not look at me. And the next thing I knew, he was engaged to Honoria.'

Mrs Budley, who had heard reports of Honoria Blessop from Sir Philip, wondered if perhaps Miss Tonks was not so silly after all, that Mr Blessop had really been courting her, but the poisonous Honoria had done something to spoil things.

She squeezed Miss Tonks's hand and said, 'We have not a bad life now. We do not have to work as servants any more either, although Sir Philip says it is good for business if we appear to work.'

'Yes, I feel so *safe*,' said Miss Tonks, 'now that we are all a family, so to speak. But sometimes I have my old dreams back, dreams where I am getting married. So ridiculous of me!'

'Not ridiculous at all,' said little Mrs Budley, and

thought of that army captain and heaved a wistful sigh.

The Duke of Rowcester was driving Miss Simms home from the Park after having taken her to see the review. Miss Simms had been just as she ought, hanging on his every word in a flattering way and looking fresh and young and extremely beautiful. He tried to persuade himself that his feeling of boredom was caused by the heat and had nothing at all to do with a longing to see a pair of bright green eyes again.

He escorted Miss Simms to her doorstep, refused an offer of refreshment, bowed over her hand and said several flattering nothings, and then, once she had gone in, climbed back into his open carriage and sat idly with the reins in his hands, staring down the street and experiencing a reluctance to go anywhere or do anything. He was expected at a ball that evening, had accepted the invitation, had assured Miss Simms that, yes, he would be honoured to dance with her. So what he should be doing was urging his carriage homeward for a bath, a change of clothes and dinner.

And yet . . . and yet . . . he could not somehow let Harriet James continue the rest of her life thinking he was too ashamed of her to introduce her to his mother. She should not have run away. She should have stayed to hear his explanation. She was a rude, hurly-burly female whose descent into trade had stripped her of the elegance of manner he expected in any female. Why should he suffer while she went about her sordid duties, as righteous as any Puritan? What would she say if she knew he had been on the brink of proposing marriage? Yes, what would she say to that?

But he had not thought seriously of proposing marriage until that evening. His heart began to lighten. It was all so very simple. But then – his spirits plunged again – what if she should refuse him? For the first time in his life he had come across a female who was not impressed by his title or rank.

On the other hand, he had no intention of going through life wondering what she would have said. Dammit, he would ask her, and if she rejected him, then he would return to the country and remain a bachelor. He was tired of London anyway.

With a set face, he told his horses to 'walk on' and drove in the direction of Bond Street.

Harriet was sitting at the dressing-table in the narrow attic room she shared with Miss Tonks and Mrs Budley, trying out a new hairstyle. If *he* called at the hotel, if *he* had the nerve to call, then he must see her at her uncaring and fashionable best. She had tried frizzing her hair in the latest fashion but it looked a mess, and with a sigh she brushed the frizz out as best she could and twirled the curling tongs into her thick tresses until she had enough curls to sweep up in a Roman style.

Then she smelled smoke and looked anxiously at the curling tongs and then at her hair, worried that she might have singed it. There was no smoke rising from her head – and yet, the smell was growing stronger.

She rose, sniffing, and then realized there was smoke creeping in long grey snakes from under the door. With a gasp she tried to open the door and found it locked fast.

Fighting down panic, she opened the window and leaned out. The street far below seemed to swim before her eyes. She grasped the sill firmly with both hands and screamed, 'HELP!' but her voice was drowned in the clamour of bells and commerce from the busy street below.

Sir Philip ambled into the hotel to find the servants huddled at the foot of the stairs. He smelled the smoke immediately. 'Fire,' said the porter. 'Gurt fire on the top floor.'

'Ring the fire bell, get everyone out,' shouted Sir Philip. 'Run to the Sun Insurance and get the engine,' he added, forgetting in his fear that he had not paid them. He scuttled up the stairs, his hand to his heart, and near the top reeled back before the intensity of the fire.

He came down again just as Lady Fortescue, Colonel Sandhurst, Miss Tonks and Mrs Budley all came in together, having met at the top of the street.

'Fire,' he said, 'in the attics.'

The guests who had come back to the hotel to change for dinner were scurrying out into the street while servants carried their belongings.

'Please God the fire engine will be here soon,' said Lady Fortescue. 'Where is Harriet?'

'My lady, Miss James was up in her room,' said a housemaid.

All of them who had meant to try to save such valuables as they could from downstairs backed out into the street and looked up.

There was Harriet's white and anxious face staring down at them.

The porter came running up. 'Sun Insurance won't come, m'lady. Says they weren't paid.'

Lady Fortescue turned and looked at Sir Philip. 'Murderer,' she said. 'You have murdered Harriet James by your theft.'

A crowd was gathering, avid faces looking up.

The duke saw the fire from the top of the street, and tossing a coin to a boy and telling him to hold his horses, he jumped from his carriage and ran towards the hotel, buffeting people aside.

He saw the faces staring up and looked up himself. Harriet!

For one dizzy moment the street spun about him and then he tore off his boots and coat, tossed aside his hat and forced his way to the hotel. Seizing the drainpipe, he began to climb.

'God in thy mercy, hear my prayer,' sobbed Sir Philip. Harriet had momentarily vanished from the window. She threw the jugs of water from the wash-stand at the now smouldering door and then returned to look down, to see if there could possibly be any way of escape.

And then the late sun slanted through the jumbled roofs onto the golden head of the duke. She held her breath. He was climbing like a cat, smoothly and effortlessly. The servants from Limmer's Hotel and the servants from The Poor Relation had formed a chain and were passing along buckets of water, men taking it in turns to dart up the hotel stairs to try to douse the inferno.

Harriet watched, her hand to her mouth. The duke leaned over from the drainpipe and grasped the attic sill. 'You must slide down my back, Miss James, and then hold on tightly round my neck and pray this drainpipe can hold us both.'

She forced herself to stay calm, not to grab wildly at him. She climbed out backwards and slid over the human ladder he formed down his back and then seized him tightly about the neck.

He found finger-holds in some crumbling masonry and worked his way along a ridge to the drainpipe and then, oh, so slowly, he began to make his way down. Above them came a great crackling roar as the roof fell in and sparks and flaming chunks of wood fell past their heads.

Down, ever downward he went, dreading all the time that the drainpipe would be torn from its moorings by the sheer weight of both their bodies. He did not once look down. Harriet had her eyes tightly closed. He was on his knees on the pavement before a wild cheer from the watchers told him they were safe.

He stood up and then clasped Harriet close to

him, kissing her hair and then her nose and then her mouth.

'Come away! Come away!' screamed Sir Philip, 'or the whole building might fall on you.'

The duke swept Harriet up in his arms and carried her to the other side of the road, where Lady Fortescue, supported by Colonel Sandhurst, was standing. Miss Tonks and Mrs Budley were very still and white, each of them glad Harriet was saved, but now terrified of the future.

The duke gently placed Harriet beside them and said, 'I must get more men organized to help with the fire.' In a daze, Harriet watched him go. She should have been thinking about what would happen to her in the future, but the only clear thought in the turmoil of her mind was to wonder whether he had noticed her new hairstyle.

The chaos slowly began to melt away several hours later. The fire had been put out, but the top two storeys of the hotel had been burnt, and guards hired by the duke were posted outside the hotel to stop any looting. Trailing into the hotel, Lady Fortescue looked wretchedly about her. She tried to tell herself that it was a miracle no one had been killed and that she should be feeling only gratitude. Even her servants, John and Betty, had been out when the fire started. Their guests had moved out to other hotels and inns. The thick smoke had crept down from the burnt upper floors and soiled everything. But at least they still had all the furniture for most of the bedrooms, the dining room, hall and coffee room, and the kitchen was completely untouched.

Their money was intact in the office safe, which Sir Philip, with superhuman strength, had dragged out into the street, saving, as Lady Fortescue acidly put it, that which was dearest to his heart.

The duke was standing in his shirtsleeves and stockinged feet, someone in the crowd having made off with his hat, coat and boots.

'What are we to do?' asked Miss Tonks helplessly. 'Where are we to go?'

'We have no guests now,' said Harriet. 'We can stay in the hotel bedrooms, which are still intact. But, oh dear, it will be hard to get money from our guests, and what we do have we will need to pay off the servants. Then how can we ever afford the repairs?'

'All of you come home with me,' said the duke. 'The guards will make sure nothing is stolen, except you had better take the money out of the safe. We will discuss what to do over supper. Betty and John have said they will also stay on guard.'

The poor relations had only the clothes they stood up in. All of them had lost little mementoes that they treasured: Harriet, two miniatures of her dead parents; Mrs Budley, letters from her husband; Miss Tonks, a pressed flower from Mr Blessop and a portrait of her father; Sir Philip, all his recently bought finery, including the new wig, which he would never wear now; Lady Fortescue, miniatures of her dead children; and the colonel, his medals, which were no doubt a melted mess somewhere in the wreckage.

The duke drove Harriet and Lady Fortescue, while the rest followed in a couple of hacks.

When Harriet saw the magnificence of the duke's town house, she thought ruefully that it was no wonder the duke should consider them all so low and disgraceful. Here were great wealth, well-trained servants and large graceful rooms, all walled away from the vulgar of London.

An efficient housekeeper took them up to their rooms, informing them that dinner would be served in an hour. Harriet sat listlessly by the window of her room, which overlooked the high wall that had originally been built when Park Lane was humble Tyburn Way, to keep the crowds going to the hangings out of sight.

For one delirious moment when he had kissed her, she thought she had come home, that he loved her and meant to marry her. But how could such as she be a duchess?

There came a light scratching at the door and then it swung open. The duke stood there. He had changed into evening dress, formal black and white embellished with diamonds.

'Miss James,' he said, 'I have a proposition to put to you.'

'Not that,' said Harriet brokenly, and covered her face with her hands and wept.

EIGHT

'Tis still my maxim, that there is no scandal like rags, nor any crime so shameful as poverty.

GEORGE FARQUHAR

Several strides and he was before her. He knelt down on one knee and gently drew her hands from her face. He took out a handkerchief and dried her tears. 'I am a clumsy oaf,' he said huskily. 'I want you to do me the very great honour of becoming my wife.'

Harriet looked at him, amazed. 'But you cannot . . . it is not possible . . . your position, your rank!'

'Damn them all. Think, Harriet, sweet Harriet, we can be married here by special licence and quit the town. It wearies me. All you have to do is say yes.'

'But . . . why?'

'Because I love you with all my heart and soul.'

'Oh.' That 'oh' was long drawn out, a mixture of rapture and pure relief. 'Yes,' said Harriet shyly.

He stood up and took her hands in his and drew her to her feet. He kissed her gently on the forehead, determined to show her his respect for her, but the siren of the bathtub rose wickedly in his mind and in a few moments both were lost in a passionate kiss of blinding intensity.

At last Harriet broke free and said raggedly, 'I am all smoky and my gown is soiled. I have not washed, and the others will be waiting for us.'

'A few moments,' he said reluctantly, 'and then we will meet again in the drawing room.'

'My love,' Harriet looked up at him. 'Why were you so ashamed of me meeting your mother?'

He laughed. 'As soon as our engagement is announced in the newspapers, you will meet my mother and you may be able to understand that I was ashamed of *her*. Hardly a worthy thought for a son, but Mama is a trifle eccentric. She and her friends would have promptly attached themselves to us for the rest of the evening, and I wanted you all to myself!'

The poor relations looked up as he entered the drawing room. They were all white with strain and fatigue. Sir Philip was sitting apart from the others, like the very pariah that Lady Fortescue had just told him he was. Footmen came in bearing decanters.

'Where is Miss James?' asked Lady Fortescue.

'Miss James will be with us presently,' said the duke.

'I am grateful to you, nephew, for all your kindness and efforts on our behalf,' said Lady Fortescue, 'but I must remind you that Colonel Sandhurst and myself consider ourselves Miss James's guardians, and now that she is under your roof, I must beg you—'

'Miss James has just done me the honour of promising me her hand in marriage,' said the duke.

Miss Tonks burst into emotional tears, Mrs Budley wept quietly and even the colonel wiped away a tear.

'It's a celebration,' said the duke gently, 'not a wake.'

Sir Philip brightened. Harriet would warn them if the duke ever noticed that necklace was a fake. He wouldn't tell her what the piece of jewellery was . . . not yet, not when she was in the first flush of romance.

Harriet came in and they dried their tears and clustered around her.

'As a wedding present,' said the duke with his arm around Harriet, 'I shall pay for the repairs to your hotel and the wages of your servants until such time as you can start up in business again.'

Before the duke's marriage announcement, both Miss Tonks and Mrs Budley might have found the courage to suggest that instead of paying for the repairs to the hotel, he present them with the money instead so that they could go off somewhere and live quietly. But Harriet was to marry a duke. Neither the stigma of trade nor her lack of dowry nor her age had spoiled her chances of happiness. Such happiness could be theirs, they thought, blind for once to Harriet's beauty.

The first shadow fell on Harriet's happiness when they were seated at supper. 'I'm sorry about the fire insurance,' said Sir Philip, 'but why did you not escape while there was still time to get down the stairs, Miss James? Were you asleep?'

Harriet looked at him in surprise and then said slowly, 'The shock of it all drove one main fact out of my head. The door was locked.'

'Are you sure?' demanded the colonel.

'Oh, yes, I wrenched and tugged at that door and it was locked fast.'

'Who would do such a thing?' cried Lady Fortescue.

'That French chef, for one,' said the colonel. 'You never told us where you found Despard, Sir Philip.'

Before Sir Philip could answer, Harriet said, 'I do not think Despard could have had a hand in it because he was frantic in his efforts to save as much of our furniture as he could. He pleaded with me to try to save his job. He appeared worried to death.

'Perhaps it was Lady Stanton,' Harriet went on. She turned to the duke. 'Do you remember at Vauxhall how she swore to get even – or rather, she said something about us being sorry we had ever crossed her?'

'I think us gentlemen had better go back to the hotel after supper,' said the duke, 'and see if we can find any evidence.'

As the duke, the colonel and Sir Philip climbed up the stairs of the hotel, they could see a full moon shining down through the charred rafters. Lady Fortescue's servant, John, led the way, carrying an oil lamp.

'Do not go too far,' warned the duke. 'The stairs are becoming unsafe.'

And so it proved. They could not risk going higher because the stairs at the top were burnt away.

'I wish I could believe that Miss James only imagined the door to be locked,' said the colonel.

'It isn't very likely,' said Sir Philip. 'Unless, of course, the wood had swollen in the heat and she thought it was locked.'

'That could well be it,' said the duke, his face clearing. 'Was there an oil lamp on the landing outside the attics?'

'Yes, but it wasn't lit until after dinner,' pointed out Sir Philip. 'Had it not been for Miss James's story, I could well believe some rival hotel set fire to the place to put us out of business, but then any arsonist would start a fire downstairs, not go up to the attics and risk discovery.'

'We'll wait until the builders get the scaffolding up,' said the duke, 'and then, although the door will have been burnt away, we might find what is left of the lock and see if the key was turned in it. Now, you all need a good night's sleep.' He turned to John, who stood patiently on the stairs, holding the oil lamp. 'John, tell the servants when they arrive in the morning that they are to keep their jobs. I will pay their wages.'

'Very good, your grace,' said John woodenly. 'Is Lady Fortescue well?'

'Yes, she has survived the shock remarkably.'

John smiled broadly, the first time either the colonel or Sir Philip had seen him smile or express any emotions whatsoever.

Sir Philip trotted downstairs, vowing to be good in the future, to be economical, and above all to insure the hotel. His great fear had been that the others would have nothing more to do with him.

And the others, as they settled down for the night, thanked God for their fortune in their different ways and resolved to be better people in future.

The colonel was to say afterwards that living in a duke's residence had gone to all their heads and made them spend like profligates. The duke's generosity seemed endless. The ladies ordered new gowns from the best dressmakers and the gentlemen kept the tailors, hatters and bootmakers busy. Harriet's wedding gown was the prime focus of interest. She was to be married in the duke's home.

The day after the announcement appeared in the newspapers, Harriet received express letters of congratulations from more relatives than she ever knew she had. And then, as she was sitting in the morning room, looking through a book of fashions, a footman announced the arrival of the Dowager Duchess of Rowcester.

'Oh, dear,' said Harriet, flustered, 'is his grace at home?'

'No, miss, his grace is supervising the repairs to the hotel.'

'Then I must see her.' Harriet stood nervously by the window.

'Where is she?' came a high, shrill voice. 'In here? I shall announce myself.'

The door opened and the dowager duchess swept in. Harriet tried not to stare at her. She was wearing a near-transparent dress damped to a scrawny body. On her head was a red wig. Her wrinkled face was rouged and painted with blanc. Behind her came two young men, tittuping on the very high heels of their boots, waving scented handkerchiefs, their faces as painted as that of the dowager duchess.

'Let me look at you,' cried the duchess. 'La, such skin and eyes. I could eat you up. What do you think, my darlings?'

To Harriet's great embarrassment, the two young men circled round her and then gave out chirruping cries of 'Ravishing! Quite divine.'

'Of course, the Stanton woman is going about telling all who will listen that you are a serving wench, which is not the case, for I checked your pedigree, my dear. Blood is important, but looks more so. Faith, had you come from the kennel I would have given you my blessing. Let me see your teeth. Ah, perfect. Have you a neat ankle?'

'I believe so,' said Harriet, backing away as the old lady showed every sign of being about to lift her skirts with her cane.

'Good, good, and here is the chilled champagne. Just the thing for the early hours of the day.'

Harriet watched as one young man snatched a bottle from the tray, opened it and poured the duchess a glass, which she drained in one gulp and then held out to be refilled. The rapid swallowing and refilling went on until she had finished the bottle.

'Now I am quite myself again,' said the dowager. 'I shall attend your wedding. So will every other relative of Rowcester's, if I am not mistaken. Such a rushed affair. Are you with child?'

'Your grace! You shock me!'

The duchess looked so highly pleased that Harriet guessed the old lady's mission in life was to shock as many people as possible.

'There now. I am sure you will breed as soon as possible. You are a bit narrow in the hips but you look strong. Now I must fly. Darlings, your arms.'

They all swept out and Harriet sank down in a chair and sighed with relief. How missish the duke must have thought her when she had been so bitterly ashamed of his having seen her naked, considering his own mother obviously paraded about London with next to nothing on.

But no sooner had Harriet begun to relax than Susan arrived, her large eyes gleaming with excitement and lips parted over white teeth. 'Do you like them?' she said, tapping her teeth with the end of her fan. 'They're real.'

'Not your own, Susan?'

'No, my own were such a dreadful colour that I had them all pulled out and got this lovely, lovely set.'

'Oh, Susan, do you never think where they came from?'

Susan wrinkled her brow. 'No, where do they come from?'

'Never mind,' said Harriet, deciding not to spoil Susan's pleasure in her new teeth by pointing out that they came from dead soldiers on the battlefields of Europe, pulled out by ghouls who took the teeth, when they had robbed everything else they could from the bodies, and sold them to London dentists.

'In any case,' said Susan, sinking down in a flurry of taffeta skirts, 'tell me all. You have caught Rowcester, and society is set by the ears. For they cannot cut a duke, you see, and Lady Stanton's revelations about me encouraging you and being your friend are falling on deaf ears, for everyone is now giving me the credit for having secured the duke for you. I am terribly in demand, and Darkwood is quite fawned on in the House and is preening himself no end and saying he always thought you a sterling lady when, in fact, he privately thought you a slut.'

And Susan laughed merrily while Harriet wondered in an exasperated way whether she ought to slap her or go and slap her husband. But Susan was rattling on.

'I know it is to be a small wedding, for Rowcester told me so, but he said that naturally I should be there. Can I be your bridesmaid?'

'I am afraid that honour goes to Miss Tonks and Mrs Budley.'

'How quaint and ungrateful of you, Harriet. But I forgive you. You must visit me often and we will both have plenty of beaux.'

'I will want no other beau but my husband,' said Harriet quietly.

'Never say you are in love with the man!'

'Very much, Susan.'

'Well, it is too bad of you to have so much, considering you are not a very deserving lady; I mean, working as a skivvy and all. Tch! What are the gods about, to pour favours in your lap and neglect me? Never mind. I cannot remain cross. Too fatiguing. Darkwood is sending you a gift. I do not like it at all. It is a large cage full of birds. But you will tell him it is pretty, will you not? Else he will sink into one of his dark moods.'

After Susan had left, Darkwood's gift arrived, which, to Harriet's relief, was not live birds but a great clockwork toy, a gilt cage full of mechanical singing birds.

In fact, presents started to pour in, and Mrs Budley and Miss Tonks volunteered to write all the letters of thanks.

'The wedding is rushing upon us,' said Harriet worriedly.

'I never see Rowcester these days. I hope he has not changed his mind. I thought . . .' She bit her lip and fell silent. She had thought they might have a quiet courtship, but marriage to a duke seemed to be a great business affair, with visits from lawyers, settlements to be signed, wills to be made; and then there was all the fuss of the wedding arrangements, and so many fittings to undergo that Harriet vowed that after her marriage, it would be years until she ordered a new gown again.

In fact, the whole of the duke's house appeared to have been turned into a vast dressmaking and tailoring establishment as the poor relations as well as Harriet were constantly being pinned and fitted.

Lady Fortescue and Colonel Sandhurst had taken it upon themselves to be Harriet's chaperones, Lady Fortescue saying sternly that any man who had his way with a maid was apt to call off the wedding. And so the duke, who longed to hold Harriet in his arms and kiss her, was constantly being thwarted in his ambitions.

Harriet grew more tense and nervous as the great day approached, seeing in the duke's set face a coldness which she feared might mean he was regretting the whole thing.

He had told her that he had not been able to find any evidence that the fire had been deliberately set, nor could he find the missing lock to her door amongst the rubble.

On the eve of her wedding, Harriet, Miss Tonks and Mrs Budley drove down to Bond Street to see what was being done. Scaffolding was erected outside and workmen were swarming everywhere. Servants were scrubbing away at the blackened walls. Soon the decorators would move in.

'Why, it will take no time at all to be finished,' said Mrs Budley, fingering the soft folds of her new muslin gown. 'It has been a holiday staying with the duke, but we are all agreed that after your marriage, Miss James, we must return here and take up residence.' She sighed. 'I had been imagining myself a society lady again.'

Harriet walked about, taking a last look around.

She would return, of course, to see them all, but she would no longer be part of this odd family of poor relations. She only hoped the duke still wanted to marry her.

On the morning of her wedding, she felt heavy-eyed from lack of sleep. Maids fussed about her, with Mrs Budley, Miss Tonks and Lady Fortescue giving advice as the white gown of Brussels lace was put on her. An emerald and diamond tiara, presented by the duke, was ready to be placed on her head.

'I always thought emeralds were unlucky,' said Lady Fortescue, 'but Rowcester said they were to match your eyes. So romantic!'

Harriet shifted uneasily under the ministrations of her helpers. She hoped the duke still felt romantic.

At last she was ready, a beautiful figure in the soft white gown and with the jewels blazing in her dark hair.

'I wish to have a word in private with Miss James,' said Lady Fortescue.

She held open the door and waited sternly until they all went out.

'Sit down, Miss James, but carefully, so you do not crush your gown,' ordered Lady Fortescue. 'Alas, your dear mother is not with you on this important day – well, not in the flesh, although she is looking down from heaven. It therefore falls to me to advise you on the intimacies of marriage.'

'I am not a young miss any longer,' said Harriet.

'But you are a virgin, yes?'

'Of course, Lady Fortescue.'

'Then you will find your first night with your husband a painful business. But gentlemen do like to think one is enjoying oneself. So you must smile and sigh despite your pain and think of the boy in the Bible with the fox gnawing at his vitals.'

'As bad as that?'

'Oh, yes, my dear. But children will be a great comfort.'

'What of romance, Lady Fortescue?'

'Unfortunately that comes before marriage, and you have not had much of the before bit. But you will be a duchess, and that must be a great delight to you. I am glad I was able to give you these words of reassurance.'

Lady Fortescue patted Harriet's hand and rose and left, leaving her feeling half bewildered, half frightened.

Five hundred guests almost managed to cram themselves into the ballroom of the duke's house, the rest spilling out into the other rooms, most of them uninvited, but when members of society sent expensive presents, they did not seem to think they would be turned away.

The weather was still very hot and Harriet hoped she would not faint during the long wedding ceremony performed by the Bishop of London. Behind her, Miss Tonks and Mrs Budley cried softly, overcome with a combination of sentimental emotion and delight in a gift from the duke of a pearl necklace for each of them.

At last they were man and wife, and stood by the door leading to the chain of saloons where the wedding breakfast was to be served. Faces passed Harriet's dazed eyes as she stood by her husband and received the guests. The wedding breakfast lasted five hours and was a rowdy affair, as everyone was crammed shoulder to shoulder and drinking far too much. The dowager duchess started to make a speech and then fell under the table. The colonel made a kind speech, and Sir Philip a vulgar one.

And then at last it was all over and carriages lined the street to take the fuddled guests away.

The duke drew Harriet's arm through his and led her up the stairs.

The poor relations stood at the bottom and watched them go.

'Let's all go for a walk in the Park,' said Sir Philip. 'I don't want to stay here and think about what they're up to. I have too vivid an imagination.'

Harriet lay stretched out in the large four-poster bed feeling like a sacrifice. Her new lady's-maid had undressed her, brushed out her hair and put her in a lacy nightgown and tied a small lace nightcap on her head. Behind the closed curtains and shutters, the sun was still shining and Harriet felt it was downright indecent to go to bed at this hour.

On a stand beside the bed, a branch of candles burnt brightly, but she did not have the courage to extinguish them.

The duke came in through a door that communicated with his room clad only in a dressing gown, which he took off and hung on one of the bedposts. Harriet took one frightened look at his naked body and closed her eyes tightly.

She felt the covers being pulled back and then felt the weight of his body next to her in the bed. Despite the heat of the day, her hands and feet were as cold as ice.

She waited for the onslaught.

But he raised himself on one elbow, and looking down at her, he began to tell her how very much he loved her, making love to her with words rather than actions until her eyes slowly opened and the cold left her body, and then, all of her own volition, she raised her hands gently to his shoulders.

The poor relations walked slowly along by the Serpentine. 'Here we are again,' sighed Lady Fortescue. 'This is where we all met.'

'I rather dread having to start up again,' said the colonel. 'In fact, I dread to think how little we might have left. Despite the duke's generosity, I fear we have been dipping into our funds. Perhaps we should not have bought Miss James such extravagant presents.'

'We could chisel some more out of Rowcester,' suggested Sir Philip.

'No, we cannot do that,' exclaimed Lady Fortescue. 'We must hit on some way of raising a little money, not as much as we needed last time, but enough to get us started and continue with the servants' wages.' She looked at Sir Philip.

'Ho, not me this time,' said Sir Philip. 'You're all so grateful to me when it suits you, but I'm a thief and a liar when it don't. Time one of the rest of you dirtied your hands.'

'I cannot find the courage,' said Lady Fortescue. 'After my last experience . . .'

'I suppose one of us should do something,' ventured Miss Tonks timidly.

Sir Philip barked with laughter. 'Oh, we don't expect you, Miss Milksop, to do anything. You're so frightened of that sister of yours, the very idea of her throws you into a fit of the vapours.'

Emboldened by all the champagne she had drunk, Miss Tonks rounded on him. 'Oh, is that so, my friend? Well, let me tell you: I shall go on a visit to Honoria and I shall take something to keep us above water. So there!'

'Bravo!' cried Mrs Budley.

'You're a Trojan,' said the colonel.

Oh dear, thought Miss Tonks, as all her Dutch courage ebbed away. What have I done?

'Like what?' asked the duke, lying languidly half across his wife's naked body.

'Lady Fortescue told me to remember the boy with the fox gnawing at his vitals.'

'Oh, Harriet.' He turned and kissed her breast. 'As bad as that?'

'Wickedly bad.'

'It gets easier.' He moved his mouth up from her breast to her lips.

'My love,' said Harriet when she could, 'what is your name?'

He began to laugh. 'It's Richard, you abandoned hussy. Do you mean you did not even know my name? I'll make you shout it to the skies.'

'How?'

'Like this, my sweet. Like this . . .'

The poor relations sat on a bench and watched their shadows growing longer in the setting sun. Somehow the old fears of what would become of them and whether they would continue to survive assailed all of them.

A reaction to the wedding and to all the luxury they had recently enjoyed was setting in.

Children's voices blown on a light breeze reached Lady Fortescue's ears and she thought of her dead children and unconsciously took the colonel's hand for comfort.

Sir Philip scowled and took Lady Fortescue's other hand in his. Miss Tonks, suddenly frightened by the temerity of what she had promised, took the colonel's hand, the one not holding Lady Fortescue's, for reassurance, and Mrs Budley's hand stole into Miss Tonks's.

And so they sat like that for a long time, hand in hand, until the sun went down and candles began to twinkle in the windows of the houses across the Park.